A STUDY IN SECRETS

LAST CHANCE
ACADEMY

BOOK
ONE

A STUDY IN SECRETS

DEBBI MICHIKO FLORENCE

ALADDIN

New York • Amsterdam/Antwerp • London
Toronto • Sydney/Melbourne • New Delhi

ALADDIN

An imprint of Simon & Schuster Children's Publishing Division
1230 Avenue of the Americas, New York, New York 10020
For more than 100 years, Simon & Schuster has championed authors and the stories they create.

First Aladdin hardcover edition March 2025
Text © 2025 by Debbi Michiko Florence
Jacket illustration © 2025 by August Zhang

For information about special discounts for bulk purchases, please contact Simon & Schuster Special Sales at 1-866-506-1949 or business@simonandschuster.com.
Simon & Schuster strongly believes in freedom of expression and stands against censorship in all its forms. For more information, visit BooksBelong.com.
The Simon & Schuster Speakers Bureau can bring authors to your live event.
For more information or to book an event, contact the Simon & Schuster Speakers Bureau at 1-866-248-3049 or visit our website at www.simonspeakers.com.
Jacket design by Heather Palisi
Interior design by Mike Rosamilia
The text of this book was set in Ten Oldstyle.
Manufactured in the United States of America 0125 BVG
2 4 6 8 10 9 7 5 3 1
Library of Congress Cataloging-in-Publication Data
Names: Florence, Debbi Michiko, author.
Title: A study in secrets / Debbi Michiko Florence.
Description: First Aladdin hardcover edition. | New York : Aladdin, 2025. |
Series: Last chance academy; 1 | Audience term: Preteens | Audience: Ages 8 to 12 |
Summary: "Twelve-year-old Meg is pulled into a mysterious treasure hunt at her new boarding school and must learn to work with her new classmates, who all have secrets of their own"— Provided by publisher.
Identifiers: LCCN 2024009952 (print) | LCCN 2024009953 (ebook) |
ISBN 9781665950473 (hardcover) | ISBN 9781665950497 (ebook)
Subjects: LCSH: Preteen girls—Juvenile fiction. | Orphans—Juvenile fiction. |
Boarding schools—Juvenile fiction. | Treasure hunting—Juvenile fiction. |
Secrecy—Juvenile fiction. | CYAC: Orphans—Fiction. | Boarding schools—Fiction. |
Treasure hunt (Game)—Fiction. | Secrets—Fiction. | LCGFT: Detective and mystery fiction.
Classification: LCC PZ7.1.F593 St 2025 (print) | LCC PZ7.1.F593 (ebook) |
DDC [Fic]—dc23/eng/20240724
LC record available at https://lccn.loc.gov/2024009952
LC ebook record available at https://lccn.loc.gov/2024009953

A STUDY IN SECRETS

CHAPTER 1

IT'S A GRAY SUNDAY as Dad drives along a road shaded by curving leafy branches that form a tunnel. It feels oddly familiar even though I've never been to upstate New York.

"It's so pretty," Dad exclaims. "Isn't this nice?"

"Hmm." Nice would be not being shipped off to Leland Chase Academy that's over four hours away from our home in Connecticut.

The road curves, and still no school comes into view. We've been driving for at least ten minutes past the big iron gates. But okay, yeah, it's pretty.

"You know what?" Dad says, his voice a bit too perky. "These woods look like the park by our house where you and Mom used to have treasure hunts. Remember?"

I remember. From the time I was five until just two years ago, Mom hid little gifts for me to find on special days: my birthday; Valentine's; New Year's; and our favorite day, the Japanese celebration of Girl's Day. In tree hollows, under bushes, behind rocks—a yellow plastic dinosaur, a small wooden box, an iridescent shell, a ten-sided die. I reach into my pocket and run my finger against the snout of an origami fox.

Dad smiles at me, thinking I'm reminiscing happily, but there's one thing I know for sure now. There are no treasures at the end of the rainbow. There's only dirt and disappointment.

"This is a really prestigious school. You're lucky they accepted you," Dad says as he pulls into a parking lot shaded by old-growth trees, the leaves just starting to change colors.

Right. Dad already told me several times how selective this school is. Special.

I turn to Dad and smile for his benefit. His face is lined with the same road map of grief I have etched onto my heart. He's hurting as much as I am, and now probably feeling some guilt, so I give him a break and try to make conversation.

"This is where we say goodbye." He turns off the engine.

"Wait, what?" I blink and look around. "You're dumping me off in a parking lot? Aren't you meeting the teacher? Or the principal? Or whatever?"

"Dr. Ward, the head of school, will meet with you and give you an orientation since you missed the first three weeks of the semester."

A sleek black limo with the Leland Chase Academy crest on it pulls into the lot.

"Listen carefully, Megumi," Dad says, using that corporate-executive voice that no one ever dares question. "If you can't stay out of trouble, if you can't make this work, you're going back to Aunt Vivian's, and you'll have to be homeschooled."

"No!" I shout, making my dad flinch. "She's a monster."

"Megumi. She's my sister."

That doesn't mean anything. Living with her the past year was the worst. She didn't make a secret of never having liked my mom. In fact, she even had the nerve to say to me that maybe Dad was better off now that Mom was dead. I will never go back there. Ever.

The limo pulls up next to us, and the driver's door opens. A white woman with blond hair pulled back into a ponytail steps out of the car. She's wearing a gray wool coat and a blue-and-gray plaid scarf wrapped around her neck.

"You need to do everything to make this work," Dad continues as he pushes the button to open the trunk of his Audi. "There are no other options. I know you want to move back home, but I'm traveling too much. It's here or Vivian's. Your choice."

It really isn't much of a choice. As the driver transfers my two suitcases and a duffel bag from Dad's trunk to the limo, Dad leans toward me and, in a rare show of emotion, wraps his arms around me, hugging me tight. "I love you," he whispers.

I know better than to let anger get the best of me. I know what it feels like not to be able to say a proper good-bye. So even though I'm upset at being sent off to a boarding school, I return his hug and say, "Love you too, Dad."

CHAPTER 2

THE DRIVER INTRODUCES HERSELF. Miss Jillian. They chat politely as she holds the rear door of the limo open for me. I slide onto polished leather seats and buckle in. Miss Jillian closes my door and takes her seat behind the wheel. Dad taps the window and waves before he hops back into his car and drives off, back home, away from me.

The driver says nothing to me. She starts the limo and pulls out of the parking lot. The paved narrow road curves left and then right. From the back seat of the limo, I keep my eyes on the sunlight sparkling through the leaves overhead. We're heading east. I guess the driver is going about twenty miles per hour. When we finally pull up in front of a huge stone building that looks like a castle, I estimate we're about three miles from the parking lot.

Mom always said that one of my strengths was being observant. I'm not sure how it will help me, since I have no intention of trying to escape. There's nowhere to go, and outdoor survival is not part of my skill set. I need to stay here. And that means not getting kicked out like I did from my last school. Cutting classes, unexcused absences, and not doing my assignments or taking tests are not options here. But ever since Mom died, I feel like school is a waste of time.

The driver turns off the engine, hops out, and opens the door for me. She didn't say anything at all the entire drive. But then again, neither did I.

I step out, feel the nip of fall in the air, and zip up my long down coat. Turning in a slow circle, I take in the sculptures, statues, and benches dotting the border of the large expanse of lawn.

"I am one of the security guards on staff," she says, finally speaking to me.

Whoa. This school has security staff? To keep students in? Or to protect them? Dad said this school has students from wealthy and influential families.

Miss Jillian continues, "Your luggage will be taken directly to your dorm room. You will meet with Dr. Ward in the main office."

She returns to the car. Something flutters at the edge of my peripheral vision. I swing left, and there, under a bush, is a flash of gray.

"Wait," I say, creeping slowly toward the bush.

My request is ignored. I hear the car door shut and the hum of the engine fading away, letting me know that the limo and Miss Jillian are gone. I drop to my hands and knees. As I crawl forward on the grass, two wide yellow eyes stare back at me.

"Well, hello there," I croon in a soothing voice.

I reach forward cautiously, not caring that I might get bitten or scratched. Then I cradle a tiny fur ball and pull it to me. The kitten is skinny with matted fur like it has been on its own for a while. I look around and don't notice a mama nearby. Once I have the kitten nestled against me, it starts purring.

Mom always wanted a cat, but Dad is allergic. If Mom were here, whispering into my ear (if I believed in that kind of thing, which I don't), she'd want me to keep it. She wouldn't want me to be alone. Besides, Dad's not around to stop me. I have to go to classes and do my assignments. Fine. But I can find other ways to be defiant. As long as I don't get caught.

I tuck the kitten into the inside pocket of my coat and stand.

Clutching the straps of my backpack, I march up the

stone steps to the imposing entrance. This place reminds me of the manors in the Jane Austen movies Mom loved. Just as I'm about to open the door, I notice a tiny hand-printed sign stuck into a planter by the entryway.

LAST CHANCE ACADEMY

I smirk at the play on the school's initials, but then I recall Dad's warning, and my smirk falls away.

I step into the largest foyer I've ever seen. A stained-glass window replicating the academy building is nestled high above an impressive staircase that branches to the left and right.

"Miss Mizuno?" An older white woman with silver hair cut in a severe bob steps into the archway. She wears a striking cobalt-blue skirt and matching jacket that's nipped in at the waist. "I'm Dr. Ward. Come with me."

She pivots and quickly strides down a short hall. I scurry after her, past carved oak double doors, through a sitting area, and into an office suite. I hope the kitten will stay quiet.

Dr. Ward sits down at an enormous desk. Behind her is a picture window framing a tall fountain in the middle of a garden that is probably spectacular in the spring, and beyond that, woods. She nods to the four red velvet armchairs in front of her desk. I take a middle one. Even though the room is warm, I keep my coat zipped up. The kitten has managed to climb out of the interior pocket and starts to inch across my belly under my coat. I gently cross my arms, trying to keep it in place.

"Megumi—" Dr. Ward starts to say.

I cut her off. "Meg." It hurts too much to hear a stranger call me by the name my mom used to call me.

Dr. Ward blinks and continues as if I hadn't spoken at all. "I've reviewed your file and your academic history. Given your mother's sudden passing, it isn't entirely surprising you struggled through your sixth-grade classes. But let me make it clear. Leland Chase Academy, while giving students a second or third chance, has high expectations of the student body. Your classmates, like you, are here for a reason. Bad behavior of any kind will not be tolerated. The rule book is in your room, and you are expected to know it front to back."

The kitten stops squirming long enough for me to pay attention. I have a feeling Dr. Ward isn't the kind of person who likes to repeat herself.

"Leland Chase Academy covers years, or grades, six through twelve. There are a total of thirty-five students currently enrolled, including you," Dr. Ward continues. "There is no way to fade into the background. Attendance and participation are mandatory. And there is a very strict schedule to follow."

Recalling Dad's warning, I grimace. Right. I need to stay out of trouble. I conveniently ignore the possible rule I'm breaking with the kitten I'm smuggling.

"Your bags have been searched and taken to your room. Your backpack, please."

When I hesitate, Dr. Ward narrows her eyes and explains. "You were given a list of prohibited items, including personal electronics. No distractions, including games and social media, or connections to former bad influences. Your laptop, tablet, phone, and chargers will be locked up. When you return home for breaks, you may have them back temporarily. We have computer labs and will provide you with a monitored school email address."

I slowly place my bag onto her desk. I have to stand in an awkward squat so the kitten won't tumble from my lap. I sit quickly as Dr. Ward removes items from my backpack. Then the kitten starts purring. Loudly. The headmaster's laser eyes snap to me.

I rub my belly. "I skipped breakfast," I say, trying to look sheepish instead of panicked. I'm pretty sure pets are not allowed.

She raises her eyebrows at me but finishes her search of my bag. Dr. Ward removes my tablet, two chargers, and my e-book reader. While she doesn't say anything, I can feel the disapproval wafting off her in waves. It's not as if I meant to break the rules. Dad told me that they have a no-electronics policy, but I assumed that meant laptops and phones. I left those behind.

Fifteen minutes later, armed with a much lighter bag and a map, I'm back in the foyer where I started.

CHAPTER 3

THE FOYER ECHOES WITH my footsteps. Where is everyone anyway? Dr. Ward made it very clear that I'm to go straight to my dorm room. The first thing I do is discreetly tuck the kitten back into the inner pocket. I study the simple map and make my way up the main staircase and turn left. This place is huge, and I look forward to exploring. In addition to my keen observation skills (as Mom always said), I have an excellent sense of direction. Mom, on the other hand, always got lost, even at the mall we always went to, and from the time I was five she would rely upon me to point us the right way.

But this is no ordinary building. Twenty minutes and four wrong turns later, I finally find the archway marked BLUE WING, the girls' dormitory wing. The first door is labeled COLETTE BEAUVOIR, RA. Kind of like the dorm monitor or boss, I guess. I walk down the strangely silent hall on a plush blue carpet. The walls are painted white with gold trim, with wainscoting decorated with wooden columns. Mom was big into English architecture, and I picked up a thing or two. There are white doors with the same gold trim as the walls, with gold-plated room numbers.

I stop at BW-27. My room. As I fumble with the key, some old-fashioned clunky thing, I glance up and notice a small rectangular silver box angled at the upper right side of the doorframe. A mezuzah. My roommate is Jewish, like my ex–best friend, Addy.

The door flies open, and I stumble into the room.

"Hi! I'm Tana Rabin, your roommate! Welcome!"

I blink, both because the room is flooded with sunlight from the large arched window and because of the brightness of Tana's voice. She has curly auburn hair and light brown eyes. Her complexion is pale, like she doesn't get outdoors much. I suspect I will soon be wearing a uniform similar to hers. Blue plaid skirt, button-down white blouse, and a gray cardigan. I'm pleased to see she's in her socks and her loafers are parked at the doorway. Even if I weren't Japanese American, I would still think wearing outdoor shoes inside a living area is gross. I kick off my black Converse All Stars and nudge them next to Tana's shoes. Not wanting to be completely rude, I mumble, "I go by Meg."

She shuts the door behind me and says, "I'm so glad you're here! Victoria was expelled two months before the end of sixth year. I was wondering if I'd get a roommate."

Not knowing how to respond, I instead take in the room. It's much bigger than I expected of a dorm room, even though I have zero experience with boarding schools. The walls are a neutral beige, but Tana's side bursts with color. Paper hearts in pink, lavender, and rose decorate the sliding closet door next to her bed, which has a very pink quilt. It looks like Cupid barfed on her side of the room. Above her desk is a shelf full of trophies and blue ribbons. Like, a LOT of trophies. I count seven before Tana tugs on my arm.

"I was a little lonesome, alone in this room," Tana says. "Come on, then, get comfy. This is your new home."

I can't decide if she's charming or annoying.

Just then the kitten once again wiggles out from the inner pocket and slips out from my coat and lands on our carpet with a soft mew.

"Oh. No pets allowed. Against the rules," Tana says.

Okay. Annoying, I decide.

She flashes me a grin. "We'll just need to be very clever about hiding him."

I take it back. Maybe Tana Rabin isn't annoying. Maybe I'm not going to completely hate it here after all.

CHAPTER 4

"FIRST THINGS FIRST." STEPPING over the kitten, who has started to explore the ruffles of her bed quilt, Tana waves at my luggage. "Unpack, and then we'll deal with the kitty. What's his . . . her name?"

I hear my mom's voice, and a name comes to me. "Sir Grey," I say. "Spelled with an *e*."

Tana nods, her curls bouncing. "The British spelling. Brilliant!"

I sit on the floor with Sir Grey in my lap and use my fingers to comb his fur. He settles in, purring loudly. It makes me wonder how long he's been on his own. Abandoned.

Tana is a whirlwind. She pushes one of my suitcases flat onto the floor and, without asking, unlatches it. She stares down at my clothes, her hands on her hips.

"Okay if I start unpacking?" she asks.

"Uh, sure." Tana seems to be a take-charge kind of person, or maybe she just doesn't want suitcases in the middle of her . . . our room. I hope she doesn't think I'm an entitled rich kid used to having a maid unpack me or something. After I place the kitten on the floor, I walk over to my other suitcase. I unpack my linens and make my bed. I would have been fine doing all of this in silence, but Tana keeps up a steady stream of commentary.

"These pants are so soft," she says as she folds them onto a shelf in my closet. "I like this T-shirt." Tana holds it up. "Is this some kind of TV show?"

They're characters from my favorite anime, but I stay silent, like it takes all my concentration to put my pillow into a pillowcase. (To be fair, it's a lot harder than you think.)

"Just so you know, I'm ranked number one in the lower school," she says, shooting me a look like she's trying to figure out if I'm competition. She has nothing to worry about, but I'm not telling her that.

When Tana's done, she closes my empty suitcase. I didn't bring a lot of clothes. The letter Dad received from the school stated that we'd have to wear a provided uniform most of the time.

"You wear a lot of black," she says. Not in a judgey tone, but still. It reminds me of Addy, former best friend.

She complained about my wardrobe after Mom died. Black for mourning. It felt right. Bright colors were for happiness and joy. All of that disappeared along with my mother. I shake my head. I don't want to think about Addy.

Tana starts to reach for my duffel bag, but I snatch it before she can touch it. She shrugs. While Tana puts my empty suitcases into the hall to be picked up, I take that moment to pull out the origami fox from my coat and tuck it into my duffel bag. I shove the bag under my bed.

Tana closes the door and smiles as her eyes find Sir Grey.

"Secrets are key here at LCA," she says. "At least secrets kept from the staff. Which includes Colette, the RA, by the way. The RA—short for 'resident advisor'—is always an eleventh year chosen because they are the ultimate teacher's pet and spy. Do not get on her bad side Also, don't trust her, because she's definitely the enemy."

That will be easy. I don't trust anyone anymore. Dad mentioned that this is a special (and expensive) boarding school for students who got kicked out of their other schools. Maybe some of the students are troublemakers, but I plan to stay off the radar.

"Jung Song is a ninth year," Tana says. "She has connections, and she can get you anything you need from the outside. As long as it's legal, because she, like most of us, can't afford to get kicked out."

"Why are you telling me this?"

Tana gestures to Sir Grey. "Cat food, litter box, litter, bowls."

"Oh!" I'm embarrassed because I should have thought of those things. There is an online school shop where students can purchase items like clothes or snacks or school supplies. While I have an account that Dad set up, he also left me with plenty of cash and a credit card (for emergencies only). But of course pet supplies wouldn't be sold at the school shop. Or allowed. "Right. Okay. How do we do this?"

"You have cash, right? Everything is cash or barter, and you do not want to barter with Jung."

"Why not?"

"She drives a hard bargain," Tana says with a sigh. "I had to drop out of the last quiz bowl so she'd have a chance of winning. And she did win."

Got it. Good to know.

Sir Grey curls up on my pillow for a nap, so it seems as good a time as any to track down this Jung Song.

Tana leads the way. We go down the hall in the opposite direction from where I came. Once at the end, we turn left down a darkened hall with wood panels.

"She doesn't live in the dorm?" I ask.

"She does, in room twenty-two, but that's right across from Colette. Jung doesn't take any unnecessary risks. She camps out in one of the state rooms to run her business and do her assignments."

We turn onto a landing with a set of dark wood stairs and head up one level. From there Tana takes the center doorway and turns. I stop and gasp.

"I know, right?" Tana whispers reverently. "I've been at LCA since the start of sixth year, and it never gets old. Welcome to the Grand Hall."

The room is cavernous, with carved wood walls lined with small statues below the plaster ceiling squares decorated with intricate designs. The statues wear grimaces, like holding wood posts running up the walls to the ceiling gives them headaches. Above the entry is a large balcony.

Tall windows bring light into the room. As I walk under a giant crystal chandelier, I spy a nook where a grand piano sits in front of a stained-glass window. Tears well up in my eyes. Mom would have loved this place. It is not lost on me, though, that I'd never be here if she were still alive.

Fortunately, Tana is leading the way, and I wipe away the tears before she turns to me.

"There's a more direct path to Jung, but I wanted you to see this room," Tana admits. "You'll have fun exploring. And getting lost. I still get lost."

I won't get lost, not once I figure this place out.

We finally enter a smaller room with windows overlooking a vast garden. The room isn't any less ornate, but set up in the center is a plain folding table, and sitting at it is a petite Asian girl. Her sleek black hair is pulled back into a short ponytail. And like Tana she wears the uniform, but her shirt collar is flipped up and the top two buttons are undone. She glances up at us with a frown. Petite *and fierce* Asian girl, I amend in my head.

"New girl," she says, nodding to me. "Cash or barter, and what do you need? And be quick. I'm studying."

CHAPTER 5

AFTER MY TRANSACTION WITH Jung is completed, Tana offers to give me a tour, but I want to explore on my own. This is the longest social interaction I've had in a year. I need some space. No offense to Tana, who seems nice, but I'm not here to make friends. I've been burned on that front.

Addy was my best friend since first grade, and we did everything together. We spent countless hours in her backyard on her play set. We learned how to ride bikes together. We walked to and from school. Mom would always have a plate of warm cookies waiting for us when we got home. And when I totally got into folding origami in third grade, Addy requested different things, a heart, a boat, a dragon, and I'd make them for her.

I was there for her whenever her brother gave her a hard time or if her parents got mad at her. I was always on her side. After my mom died, she was patient with me for all of two weeks after the funeral. Addy told me I wasn't any fun anymore, and then she started hanging out with other girls. The only good thing about being sent away to live with Aunt Vivian in sixth grade was that I didn't have to be ignored by Addy anymore.

I hope to figure out the layout of the school quickly, but this manor is a mysterious maze. I feel lucky to find my way back to the girls' wing because I never come across the same set of stairs twice, except for the main stairs. I check my watch as I walk down the darkened hall. The watch belonged to Mom and before that to her mother, and while smart watches aren't allowed, I'm able to keep this one. I'm surprised to see I've been gone for over three hours!

I open the door to my room. (Feels strange to call it that.) Tana is hunched over her desk but turns to me with a smile when I shut our door.

"I'm glad you're back! I worried you got lost," she says.

Sir Grey mews as he stretches on my pillow. Then he walks primly over to the edge of my bed. I scoop him up, and he purrs loudly.

Tana points to a paper bag in front of my closet. "Speedy delivery today," she says. "Jung says she'll get real kitty litter for the next order. For now it's fine gravel from the gardening shed."

We agree to put the litter box (the bottom half of a small plastic storage bin) in my closet, which runs the length of the room next to my bed. Tana assures me that actual room checks, outside of quick peeks for evening curfew and Sunday morning room cleaning, are very rare, though that's how Victoria, her former roommate, got caught with contraband and expelled. I'll clean his litter box daily to keep the smell from being noticed, and Tana tells me about the dumpster behind the school kitchen that's perfect for getting rid of contraband trash.

"You're back just in time for dinner," Tana says, standing and stretching.

"Oh, I'm not really hungry." The last thing I want is to deal with a cafeteria and a crowd.

"You're not allowed to miss dinner," she says. "They take attendance, and you have to either be severely ill with a note from the school nurse or have an approved excuse from a teacher."

Fantastic.

A sharp rap sounds on our door, and we both startle. I gently shove Sir Grey into my closet, where I've already placed a cat bed (my extra pillow), and hope he doesn't protest or make any noise. Tana opens our door.

A girl with wavy brown hair and wearing the academy

uniform steps in like she owns the place. I notice that her knee socks are cobalt blue, unlike Tana's gray, and pinned to her gray cardigan is a badge with the LCA crest. Her eyes are sharp as they swoop around our room. Thankfully, Sir Grey remains silent.

"Megumi Mizuno, why are you not in uniform?" she barks at me.

Tana jumps in. "Colette, she literally just got here."

Colette, the RA, the enemy. Tana said I have to stay on the RA's good side. I force a smile, something I haven't had to do in a long while. "Dr. Ward said my uniforms would arrive by this evening."

Colette narrows her eyes at me like I'm being smart with her. That makes no sense, since I'm using my non-snarky voice and only telling her what Dr. Ward said.

"Fine. Let's go," she says, opening our door wide and gesturing to the hall.

"Where are we going?" I ask.

"Dinner!" Colette sighs loudly. "Have you not reviewed the schedule yet?" She turns to Tana. "I'm disappointed. You need to do a better job of mentoring a new student. Or you'll be without a roommate again."

I don't understand why Colette is being so harsh, but I decide right then and there that I don't like her at all.

CHAPTER 6

"SERIOUSLY, READ OVER THE rule book. I'll be testing you," Colette states as she leads us out of the girls' wing and down the main staircase. "Be in uniform at all times. Only exception is in the evenings after dinner and some outdoor school activities. Don't be late to class. I'll hear of it. And if Tana hasn't already told you, I am generous with demerits."

I scurry to keep up with her as we go around the staircase to a hallway tucked behind it.

"I can see from your face that you have no clue about demerits. I'd give you one for not knowing, but because I'm nice, I'll give you one week to memorize the rule book."

I hold back a scoff because Colette is anything but nice.

Tana is breathing hard as she tries to keep up with our speed walking.

We finally reach a large room set up with two long rows of dining tables draped with white tablecloths, surrounded by red velvet chairs. On the ceiling is a painting of blue sky, white clouds, and cherubs. Fancy gold decorations border the tops of the walls, which are papered in cream and gold. This is not the cafeteria I expected.

Almost every chair is occupied by a student, and the first thing I notice is that this is a very diverse student body. At my old schools most of the students were white. For the first time ever I feel like I might fit in, or at least blend in. The second thing I notice is that the room is eerily silent. Some students are talking, but in whispers.

"Megumi Mizuno, new student, seventh year," Colette announces, and thirty-two pairs of eyes turn to us. "Make sure she knows the rules."

Tana guides me to two empty seats toward the center of one of the long tables. We sit across from two Asian boys in dark blue blazers, white button-down shirts, and plaid blue-and-gray ties.

"We sit with our class," Tana says softly as I take my chair. "There are four of us in seventh year."

Four of us! And of the four, three of us are Asians. I know I shouldn't hyper-focus on this, but I can't help it. I had only one Asian classmate at the school I went to for sixth grade. It was annoying because other people either thought we were related (he was Vietnamese, and we looked nothing alike) or assumed we'd make a cute couple (we didn't even know each other).

As the kitchen staff enters carrying trays with plates of food, the conversation in the room rises a little in volume. I'm relieved that we are not required to eat in silence. Not that I want to have conversation, but the silence was a little weird.

"Hi, Megumi. I'm Ryan Hsieh," the Asian boy across from Tana says with a cheery smile. His black hair is swooped off his forehead and trimmed neatly around his ears. I'm not so closed off that my heart doesn't bounce. He's very pretty. I'm so distracted by his good looks that I forget to correct him, but Tana jumps in.

"She goes by Meg," Tana says, jostling me out of my daze. She nods to the boy next to Ryan. "And this is his roommate, Zane Yoshikawa."

I turn to the other Asian boy, and this time my heart leaps because of his glare. His dark hair falls into his eyes and curls around his ears and at his neck. His tie is slightly askew, and the knot is loose. I nod at Ryan and then quickly at Zane and am grateful when a dinner plate is placed in front of me.

Tana and Ryan keep up a steady chatter, both of them giving me a rundown of what my week will look like. We have all our core classes together every morning, and independent study and study hall in the afternoon. Dr. Ward gave me what she called a generous three weeks to choose my independent study topic. Turns out Tana's is computer programming.

Zane keeps his attention on his food the entire time, not engaging at all, which normally I would appreciate, since I, too, plan to keep to myself. But honestly? He's rude.

Suddenly the hairs on the back of my neck tingle as Ryan's eyes focus on something behind me.

"Don't think because you're new or starting late that I'll give you any breaks," Colette says, her breath hot in my ear. "And you'd better be in uniform when I see you in the morning."

When dinner is over, Tana and I push our chairs back. I take a sweeping glance around the room. Colette sits with the other eleventh years, but it's as if there's an invisible barrier around her, and no one seems to be talking to her.

I will do my best to avoid the RA and her demerits, but I have a feeling it won't be easy.

CHAPTER 7

THE SCHEDULE ISN'T THAT hard to learn, even if it's unlike any I've ever had. Every day starts with Life Skills class, which doubles as homeroom. Our teacher is Ms. Sheth, a South Asian woman who looks like she just graduated from college. She is almost as new to the school as I am. She seems low-key, and I like her right away.

Mondays and Wednesdays are one set of classes, and Tuesdays and Thursdays are another. Fridays are test prep and test days. It's strange to attend classes with only Tana, Ryan, and Zane, but at least for the first week things go smoothly.

I feel the most pressure in the afternoons, when all the other students are doing their independent studies. I don't have a lot of time to figure out something I have to devote every afternoon to for the rest of my career here at Leland Chase. Good thing I have no intention of staying longer than this school year. I want to convince Dad to let me move home with him for eighth grade, if not sooner.

Friday afternoons, after extracurricular classes, are for "school projects," which is a fancy way of saying "free labor." I'm assigned to the gardens. Mr. Roberts tells me to pull up all the old tomato plants from the beds. I know nothing about plants, but I try my best. But my best turns out to be yanking out all the lavender, which apparently are not supposed to be pulled. (In fairness, it would have been nice if he had pointed out what tomato plants look like.) I'm told to instead sweep all the pathways.

After dinner I'm ready to collapse. I hope to spend most of the weekend sleeping. I've been keeping up in my classes and managed not to get into any trouble. My plan to stay enrolled has been a success, at least for week one.

But I'm thwarted before I even reach my room, when Colette blocks the hall. She waves Tana through but stops me.

"What are activity nights and when do they take place?" she snaps at me.

"Planned school activities like movie night or game night. Attendance is mandatory in the Green Room. They happen every Friday and Saturday evening." I've been expecting this all week, and if Colette thought I'd be easy to bully, she is wrong.

"How many demerits result in detention?"

"Three in a month." I don't elaborate that I know that the demerits she gives don't carry the same weight as those given by a teacher. I try to get around her, but Colette sidesteps, easily blocking my path.

"And for expulsion?"

"Five in a month." Again, I don't explain that the five demerits only mean a threat of expulsion. The rules clearly state that it's not automatic and the student's records will be reviewed in a meeting with a parent or guardian.

"What's on page 115 of the rule book?" Colette leans against the wall with a satisfied smirk. She thinks she's bested me. She doesn't know me at all.

"There is no page 115. The rule book only goes up to page 100." I smile back at her.

Colette straightens with a glare. "Don't think you've won."

I step forward, and this time she lets me pass. I feel her eyes on me all the way to my room. After I open my door and close it with a quiet click, I press my back against the door and sigh quietly.

"That bad?" Tana asks, spinning her desk chair to face me. She studies pretty much all the time, which makes her my ideal roommate. No "Let's hang out and be best friends" vibe from her, but also no "You disgust me and I hate being around you" vibe either. I've already figured out that Tana is very competitive. She likes to be first, have the highest score, and be the best at everything. All the trophies and ribbons that she keeps on display are for first places only.

"Nothing I can't handle," I say, kicking off my Converse. Fortunately, as long as our footwear is black or navy blue, we can wear any flat shoes. Getting to keep a small part of myself gives me comfort.

My first Friday activity night is a movie, and I'm relieved. I can just sit there, not talk to anyone, and stare at the screen. It's an action flick that I wanted to see with Dad, but of course he was so busy traveling that we didn't see any movies together at all. I wonder if Dad will remember our phone call. We agreed on every Saturday evening at seven, allowing me to leave dinner a little early. I have to take calls in Dr. Ward's sitting room on an actual old-fashioned landline phone.

When we get back to our room, we change into our pj's. Sir Grey curls up on his pillow in my closet just as Colette knocks on our door at curfew. Tana opens it. Colette steps in, takes a quick glance, and steps out, moving on to the next room.

At least tomorrow is Saturday. I can sleep in and wander around the manor and the grounds in the morning. Saturday mornings and all day Sunday, with the exception of room cleaning, are the only times we don't have scheduled activities. I made it through my first week at

Last Chance Academy with little drama (drama courtesy of Colette) and without getting kicked out (despite Colette's efforts).

I crawl into bed, and Sir Grey hops up onto me. He purrs, making my chest rumble. I stroke his soft fur, happy that I at least have him. Pets don't disappoint you. Pets don't abandon you. Not like people.

"Good night," Tana says as she reaches over to her lamp.

Just as Tana switches off the light, a flash of silver slides under our door.

CHAPTER 8

TANA HOPS OUT OF bed and follows me to the door. She turns on a mini flashlight she sometimes uses when she studies under her covers after lights-out. Sir Grey remains curled up. Lucky for us, he's truly mellow and loves to sleep.

On the floor are two silver envelopes. I turn one over. In curly script is written "Tana Rabin." I flip the other, and my heart leaps when I see "Megumi Mizuno" written in the same handwriting. Tana and I lock eyes, and in the dim light I can see her hesitation.

I shrug, but a trickle of anticipation runs through me. After a long week of schoolwork and with a long weekend of nothing planned, this is intriguing.

"What if it's something bad?" Tana says.

"So what? It's still interesting." I slide my fingernail under the flap of my envelope and unseal it. Inside is a stiff piece of charcoal-colored paper printed with silver ink. I skim the note.

You are cordially invited to play . . . and win an all-expenses-paid luxury vacation to Newport Beach, California, over winter break! (You choose your chaperone.)
There are only three rules:

1. *For the entirety of the game, no matter if you are playing or eliminated, if any administrator, staff, RA, or 12th-year student discovers what you're up to, the game is off. Don't ruin it for others.*
2. *There are ten silver envelopes hidden in a book. Take only one. Ten participants will move on to the next round.*
3. *Have fun!*

Small print: good luck.

"What is this?" Tana whispers, reading the same words on her invitation.

I smile. "It's a treasure hunt."

In the dim moonlight shining through our windows, I see Tana crinkle her brows in thought.

"Is this a Leland Chase Academy tradition or something?" I ask. Or hazing? I've read stories like that, where newbies were dared in challenges to become accepted. Is this place some sort of secret society?

Tana shakes her head. "No. I mean we didn't have one of these last year, at least. And it doesn't sound like it's run by the school."

Interesting. Very!

CHAPTER 9

WHILE WEEKEND DINNERS ARE mandatory, weekend breakfasts and lunches are buffet-style, and attendance is optional, so I take full advantage. I sleep in till ten, and when I finally roll out of bed, of course Tana is already gone and probably at the computer lab.

Tana and I didn't discuss the invitation further last night, so I have no idea if she's going to do it. I bet she will. It's a competition, so she can't resist.

I'm good at treasure hunts. Really good. Even if the school isn't running it, and even if this truly is some secret game, the idea of playing would normally be very exciting to me. But treasure hunts remind me of Mom, and thinking of her, remembering the loss of her, hurts too much. I can't. I just can't. I won't.

Also, it's clear from the rules that getting caught can lead to trouble. And I can't risk trouble. I have to stay enrolled here. A tiny tickle of regret threads through me, because this would be a good diversion. But ending up back at Aunt Vivian's would be the worst. I have to try to resist.

That's why I'm not going to do the mysterious secret treasure hunt. If I get caught, I'll probably get kicked out, or at least get some of those demerits Colette is determined to hand out. Plus, what if this is a mean trick of Colette's to get students in trouble? She seems to thrive on fear. It doesn't matter. I'm staying. For now.

I feed Sir Grey and clean his litter box. As I have every day, I tuck the trash bag into my backpack to toss into the kitchen dumpster. This kitten is worth the extra work.

After I dump the trash, I head back into the manor determined to explore. The school schedule during the week leaves very little free time for anything, and because I haven't yet chosen my individual study, I'm stuck sitting in Ms. Sheth's classroom, being babysat while I research my choices and while she preps for the science classes she teaches.

I go straight to the Grand Hall, the huge ornate room Tana took me to my first day. I want to find a way onto the balcony. But when I get there, two other students are in the room. Liam Parkison, a white eleventh-year guy, and Winsome Williams, a Black eighth-year girl who often sits next to me at mealtimes. It was easy for me to learn everyone's name, since there are only thirty-five of us and during mealtimes we sit with our classes. I only needed to ask Tana once who was who. Winsome nods at me and then returns to looking through a stack of books on a table.

I'll explore this room later, when I don't have an audience. I walk through the Grand Hall and get to the room where Jung Song camps out. I notice she has stacks of books on her table, and she, like Winsome, is flipping through them quickly. When she catches me peeking, she shoots me a glare and I duck back out.

It doesn't take a genius to figure out what's going on. I swing by the library, and it's filled with students, every single one of them flipping through pages of books at random. Everyone is looking for silver envelopes.

"What's going on in here?" Colette's voice shatters the silence as she pushes past me into the library.

Every girl in the library freezes, knowing full well what Colette is capable of. The two boys in the room, Owen Reyes and Gavin Tran, both tenth years, casually sit down.

"What do you mean?" Gavin says. "We're studying."

"Gavin," Colette says in a warning voice. "This library has never had this many students in it at once, even during finals."

I take that moment to escape the library. I'm glad I wasn't caught with a book in my hand. Which sounds really silly when you think about it. I mean, why can't students be in the library looking at books? And why does Colette always have to be on the prowl? At least I'm not the only one she stalks.

"Hey!" I jump guiltily as Colette corners me in the hall. "What were you doing in the library?"

"Looking for a place to study," I say, hitching my backpack. "But it was too crowded."

Colette narrows her eyes at me. "There's something funny going on. I'm going to find out. If you know something, you should tell me."

"I know nothing."

"That is probably true." Colette sniffs and then stalks downstairs like she's on a mission.

Fine by me. I just want to stay out of trouble.

But then, trouble always seems to have a way of finding me.

CHAPTER 10

ALL I WANT IS to get away from Colette. I take the flight of stairs up to the fourth level, where I haven't been yet. The last step before the landing creaks loudly, making me flinch.

Down the dark and narrow hall is an empty room that overlooks the front of the school, with a view of the long driveway that first brought me here almost a week ago. I drop my backpack onto the floor and stare out the window. A group of students kick a soccer ball on the front lawn. We have gym after lunch on Saturday, which is about all the physical activity I can take. But watching the students high-fiving, laughing, and shouting makes me feel very isolated and alone.

I circle the room, looking for a place to sit, but there is nothing here. No tables. No chairs. Just an empty room that echoes like my empty heart. I slump against a wood-paneled wall and slide down onto the floor.

A birthday memory comes unbidden.

"Megumi! Here's your clue!" Mom handed me an origami fox.

I unfolded it carefully because I wanted to put it back together and keep it. I read out loud, slowly, since in the first grade I was still learning words. "I'm rich with many rings, but they are not to wear on your fingers."

I glanced at Mom, who sat on the picnic blanket where we had just finished our lunch of Spam musubi. It was a warm spring day, and the smell of lilacs, Mom's favorite flower, wafted through the air. She smiled and nodded at me, encouraging me. I thought hard. Rings but not on fingers. I stood and started to walk around the park, hoping for a clue. And then I saw it. The tree stump. The other day Dad had shown me the rings on the stump and told me that by counting them you could tell how old the tree was. I broke into a run, Mom close behind me. When I got to the stump, I searched. Beneath a small pile of leaves, I found a yellow plastic dinosaur. "I got the treasure!"

Mom laughed in my ear as she scooped me up into a hug. "My smart and observant treasure hunter," she said.

I shake my head, bringing myself out of the memory. I reflexively reach into my pocket but remember that I put the origami fox into my duffel bag. I carried the fox with me the entire year in sixth grade, as if Mom's spirit was in that paper. Which is silly, I know, because she gave me so many little treasures, so many clues, and I kept them all. But that origami fox was the start of my origami obsession. Mom and I used to fold origami all the time until I got good enough (better than her) to make them on my own. But I don't fold origami anymore.

I lean my head back against the wall harder than I intend, thwacking it. My head sounds hollow. No. Wait. Not my head.

I turn to the wall and knock. It sounds strange. I scoot over to the next panel and knock. Solid. I stand up and scrutinize the wall I was leaning against. My section of the wall has a pair of columns bordering it. I lean down. Next to the right column closer to the floor is a brass ring. Like a door knocker. I pull on it. Nothing. I tug harder. It doesn't budge.

None of the other sections of the walls have a brass ring. It has to be for something other than decoration. I knock on the wall again. I press my ear to the wood. I hear nothing, but I do feel something. A cool, steady stream of air wafts across my face. There, nestled on the outside edge of the right-hand column, is a tiny brass oval. At the center is a round opening. When I press my eye against it, I don't see anything, but I can feel the air coming through it. A keyhole? A keyhole!

I pat my empty pockets and then scramble to my backpack and drag it over, looking for something, anything that might fit into that hole. I try my pen, but it's too thick. I groan quietly. But then I get another idea. I run my fingers along the edges of the wall, trying to find a grip, and when my fingers slide into a small crevice, I dig in harder and feel the wall move just slightly. My heart pounds with anticipation.

I keep tugging on the wall with my right hand, and with the other I grab the brass ring. This time it turns, like a doorknob. And slowly the wall pulls away, swinging open like a door.

Behind the wall is a small room filled with boxes. I step in, and the air smells musty. There is a stack of old chairs to my right, and in front of me is a shelving unit. I poke around, moving boxes and peeking into them. Old kitchen equipment. More shelves line the rest of the cramped space, and I continue to look inside boxes. Cracked dishes and mugs with the Leland Chase Academy crest. Stained tablecloths and dented napkin rings. At the very back is an enormous trunk. When I try to open it, I discover it's locked with a padlock. Strange. Everything else here is pretty much junk. What's in the trunk?

Suddenly I hear a telltale creak. I scramble out of the room and push the wall closed, pressing against it with my back. Just as the wall clicks into place, Colette strides into the room. I know I look suspicious, standing with my back to the wall, but I don't move a muscle.

"Why are you up here?" she asks, her eyes roaming the room.

"I told you, I was looking for a place to study."

"Here?"

"It's empty and quiet." I slide down to the floor and grab my backpack, glad I moved it closer to me. I pull out my social studies textbook and flip it open.

"I'm watching you," Colette says as she leaves the room.

She stalks out, and I grin, feeling triumphant like I scored a victory against her. The more she harasses me, the more defiant I feel. She may think she's intimidating me, but instead of feeling bullied, I feel challenged. A thrill runs through me, and I wonder if there are other secret rooms in the manor.

It's then that I realize why I was digging through the boxes in the secret room. I was looking for books. I was looking for a silver envelope.

I am treasure hunting once again.

CHAPTER 11

MONDAY MORNING I SLIDE into my seat in Life Skills just as the chime sounds, letting us know the school day has begun. Ms. Sheth hasn't arrived yet.

I spent the rest of the weekend searching but came up empty. The library always had at least one other student combing through books. I don't want anyone to know I'm looking for an envelope.

I wonder if the other seventh years are playing. Ryan flashes me a smile when he notices me looking at him, and I quickly glance away, feeling my cheeks burn. To my left, Zane rests his head on the desk, turned away from me. He never says anything in class unless he's called on, but he always has the correct answer. He gives it like he's put out, though.

"Where is Ms. Sheth? She's never late." Tana leans forward past Ryan to talk to me. All four of us sit in the front row.

Ryan tips his chair back, balancing precariously on the back two legs.

"You're going to break your neck," Tana says matter-of-factly.

"Not likely," he says, but he tilts forward again, putting all four chair legs firmly onto the floor. "Anyone get anything interesting on Friday night?"

Zane lifts his head as Tana raises her eyebrows at me, silently asking if we should tell Ryan. I shrug. I mean, it's obvious to me that the rest of the school got the same invite, but maybe neither Ryan nor Tana skulked around the manor like I did all weekend.

"Yes," Tana says.

Since Ryan and Zane are roommates, I suspect that they both have envelopes. For a moment I get distracted, wondering what it must be like in that room. Zane is so unfriendly, so sullen, and Ryan is the exact opposite. Do they talk at all?

"Did you find one of the ten envelopes?" Ryan asks, interrupting my thoughts.

"Did *you* find one?" I counter. Ryan's smile is so bright and warm that I almost spill everything I know to him, but I manage to instead ask, "Do you guys think this is being run by the school?" Even though Tana said this wasn't done last year, maybe the boys know something else?

Ryan laughs. "Doubt it. They're not known for being fun."

And it strikes me that of course that's what this is. Fun. Most of the students here can afford luxury vacations, probably to locations more fabulous than California. It's fun for me too, but it's more than that. Treasure hunts connect me to Mom, but if I win, it will be a chance for me to bond with Dad. Going on vacation with him, just the two of us. And maybe I can convince him to let me move home. This prize could be the key to my getting home.

Ms. Sheth scurries in. "Sorry, sorry!" she says, out of breath. "The staff meeting went long, and then I got turned around."

I smile to myself. Even the teachers get lost around here, at least the newer ones.

Today, as she has every day, Ms. Sheth is wearing leggings and a kurti top, this one bright turquoise. She strides to her desk, and for a moment I'm envious that the teachers don't have to wear uniforms. Sometimes I miss the bright colors I used to wear before I switched to black. And now I wear the somber gray-and-blue uniforms of LCA.

"Today is Founder's Day," Ms. Sheth says with a smile. She leans on the edge of her desk. "The new teachers and staff were given the history of Leland Chase Academy. I suppose you all already know it."

48

Heads bob, but I shake mine.

"Ah, Ms. Mizuno, that's right. You're new just like me," Ms. Sheth says. "A review, then, for Ms. Rabin, Mr. Yoshikawa, and Mr. Hsieh. Leland Chase was a very wealthy man, making his money in real estate in Manhattan in the early 1900s. He had an obsession with his English background, so he built this manor, based on English architecture.

"But when the stock market crashed in 1929 . . ." Ms. Sheth pauses and says, "Note that for your social studies class."

Tana scribbles it into her notebook while Zane makes a sound under his breath.

"Anyway, Leland Chase lost all his money and went bankrupt," Ms. Sheth continues.

Zane mumbles, "Serves him right." But I think I'm the only one who hears him.

Ryan jumps in. "Leland Chase died suddenly, maybe from shock, right after that stock market crash. The family lost this place, even though his two sons tried to keep it in the family."

"Right." Ms. Sheth flashes a pleased smile at Ryan. "He was unable to pay the taxes, and it was turned over to the state and forgotten, until two wealthy families got together to buy it at a very reduced price in 1965, to turn it into a private boarding school."

"Why?" I ask.

"Cuz their kids were like us," Ryan says. "Trouble-makers who couldn't stay in school. Money solves every-thing, right? Buy and make a school so your rich kids can still graduate and get an Ivy League education and take over family businesses or whatever."

I'm surprised Ryan sounds angry, when so far he's always had a cheerful attitude. It makes me wonder why he's here.

"I suppose that's one way to look at it, but this school does serve a purpose, and the standards of education are high here," Ms. Sheth says. "Anyway, in the 1990s the school was taken over by a private trust and a board of directors. Today, while the trust and tuition cover all the basics of the school, LCA is very reliant upon donations."

"What happened to Leland Chase's sons?" I ask.

"I don't know. I suppose they moved on," Ms. Sheth says. And then she gets a gleam in her eye. "You can research that, Ms. Mizuno."

"Wait, what?"

Ryan snickers.

"It's not an assignment," Ms. Sheth says, "but since you missed the first three weeks of the semester, I can offer you some extra-credit points. You don't have to do a formal report. An informal oral presentation would suffice."

"I'll do it!" Tana nearly shouts.

Ms. Sheth laughs. "I may be new, but I have heard

about you from the other teachers, Tana, and I doubt very much you will need extra credit."

Like I do? I don't need or want extra credit.

"Again," Ms. Sheth says to me, "only if you feel like it."

Right. I won't feel like it. I have enough work to do, catching up in my classes. I just need to maintain a B average to stay enrolled. And not get kicked out. I would rather be living with Dad. But this is better than living with Aunt Vivian.

I know I'm making a bad decision by doing this treasure hunt, risking my enrollment. But it's as if Mom has been training me for this all along, and instead of feeling sad about missing her and about missing treasure hunting with her, I feel like she's with me in spirit, cheering me on.

Time is ticking. I need to find an envelope.

CHAPTER 12

THERE IS ZERO TIME for real conversation during the school day. Before I got the treasure hunt invitation, I didn't care about that. But now I need information. I need to know who I'm up against. I wait until lunch to talk with my classmates.

Ryan is cagey but chatty. Zane just shovels food into his mouth like he thinks we might not get another meal ever. But I can tell he's listening. He's sneaky. I'll have to remember that. I give nothing away, while seeming to be forthcoming.

"The paper didn't come from the school, I don't think. Too fancy," I say.

"How do you know?" Zane says. "It could have come from a student's personal stash or maybe a teacher."

I'm so surprised that Zane has said anything that I'm speechless. But Ryan is not. Which makes me think they do talk in their dorm room.

"I don't think a teacher would bother. I mean, it's a pretty pricey prize by anyone's standards." Ryan plays with a French fry, dragging it back and forth through a glob of ketchup. "Maybe one of the RAs?"

"No way," Tana says. "Colette is not that good an actress. She knows something is up, and she's definitely trying to figure it out."

"All the more reason to keep this quiet," I say. "If she finds out, it's over."

"So why do you think twelfth years are excluded?" Ryan asks.

"Probably because they won't care about vacation since they're graduating," Tana says. "They're swamped with senior projects and college applications. They're almost out of here. Why would they risk getting caught and kicked out?"

"Or maybe one of them is running it," Zane says softly.

"What would be the point? Like Tana says, they're almost out of here. Anyway, who cares who's running it, as long as one of us wins?" Ryan says. He turns to me. "You want to work together?" He smiles, and I'm glad I'm sitting, since my knees feel melty. It's like he's used to getting his way with that smile. But I'm not that easily swayed.

I shake my head. "I think there's more of a chance of being caught if we're seen together all the time."

"Okay, but we can still share information," Ryan says, his eyes on me.

Tana nudges my leg with hers, but I don't know if she means to tell me to disagree or agree. It doesn't matter, because I'm not a team player. I shrug and for the rest of the meal focus on eating quickly. I have an idea that might get me ahead of everyone else.

After lunch I head straight to Ms. Sheth's room.

"Ms. Mizuno," Ms. Sheth says with a smile. "Good afternoon."

"Hi," I say without sitting down. "I appreciate you trying to help me figure out my independent study project, but I feel like I'm wasting your time."

"Oh, no, Meg," she says, shaking her head. "This is part of my job, and I enjoy spending time with you."

"Thanks," I say, thinking quickly. "But what if I take time to explore? Check out the library, walk the grounds. Maybe I'll get an idea that way?"

Ms. Sheth purses her lips. "That could work. Some people think better that way."

To my relief, after a beat, she nods. "Okay, let's give it a try, shall we? I'll write you a note in case you get stopped. And hopefully you'll figure out what your independent study will be."

I have to. I meet with Dr. Ward next week. She won't give me an extension. She said as much when I showed up to take my call with Dad on Saturday evening. Thinking of Dad, my heart twists. Our call was super short because of course Dad was on his way to the airport for yet another business trip. He hardly ever traveled when Mom was around. It was always the three of us, together. But after Mom died, he changed. I did too. But while I want us to be a team of two, he seems to want to fly solo. I miss him. I miss Mom, too, but there isn't anything I can do about that. She's gone.

I head to the library first. I have until three o'clock, when study hall starts and students are likely to be studying or checking out books. But during independent study, as I suspected, no one is here. I start flipping through books, shelf by shelf. It's tedious and I'm running out of time. Maybe the book is more cleverly hidden. I climb onto a step stool and run my hand across the tops of the bookshelves. But after checking every nook and cranny, under tables and chairs, I come up empty.

When I arrive at the dining room for dinner, Ryan nearly pounces on me the second I sit down.

"Anything?" he asks.

"You?"

Instead of giving me grief for not answering him directly, he laughs. "I like you, Meg."

Before we can continue, a triangle sounds from the front of the room, signaling an announcement. My heart sinks when I see Colette instead of one of the teachers standing there ringing it. The room grows silent. Oliver Smythe, the boys' RA, stands up to join her.

"Go, Oliver!" Mateo Davis, Oliver's boyfriend, calls out. Students laugh quietly.

Colette's face goes from stony to resigned. I've learned that Oliver is a very popular RA. Beloved. While he goes by the rule book, he's also very chill. Unlike Colette, he's not out to get everyone. I wish he were our RA instead.

Once everyone settles down, Oliver goes through the upcoming week's schedule and activities. "On Saturday afternoon, gym rotation continues with tenth-, eleventh-, and twelfth-year students with Coach Ken Jordon for swimming. The rest of the girls will meet with Arianna Hernandez for track, and the boys with Roger Jensen for soccer drills. The schedule will be posted on the RAs' doors as usual."

At least at LCA we only have enforced physical activity once a week, even if it's for two and a half hours.

"And I have something fun to announce," Oliver says with a smile. "For Saturday evening activity we have a doubleheader. First a hike with nature expert Carole Rogers. After that we will have a nighttime star walk led by Dr. Daniel Chen, a renowned astronomy expert visiting us from Canada."

That gets almost everyone talking. I'm less enthused. Like I mentioned before, I'm not really an outdoor person, but it will be nice to get out of the manor at least.

When the servers come out with trays of food, Colette adds, "If any of you are involved in unsanctioned activity, be aware that it is cause for demerits. Oliver and I will be watching."

From behind Colette, Oliver rolls his eyes.

I hold in a grin. If anything, it will be fun to thwart Colette.

CHAPTER 13

IT'S THURSDAY AFTERNOON AND I'm making my way through the conservatory. I have pretty much checked most of the manor, at least the places where students can go. I doubt the envelopes are hidden in places forbidden to students. Still, I haven't found anything.

"There you are." Ryan enters the conservatory through the outside door.

"What are you doing here?" I brush the dirt off my hands. Not that I expect a book to be buried in the dirt, but I'm not going to leave any stone unturned. Literally.

"I could ask you the same." As usual, he's dressed immaculately. His shirt is pressed, the knot of his tie is perfect, and his jacket is buttoned. While all of us get our uniforms cleaned by the school, Ryan's shirts always look crisper.

"Do you get special cleaning services or something?" I ask.

His eyes crinkle as he grins. "You been checking me out, Meg?"

I frown, despite the warm flush creeping up my neck. "No. Just observant."

"There's a laundry room in the basement," he says with an embarrassed shrug. "I like my shirts to be ironed perfectly."

"You iron your own shirts?"

"Mm-hmm." Ryan smiles. "Have you found anything?"

This time I'm honest because I'm frustrated. All I've found is a tiny fairy garden tucked behind some plants. I even examined it very closely in case there was a miniature book. (There wasn't.) Why haven't I found an envelope yet? Could it be that they've all been claimed by now?

"I'm striking out left and right," I admit.

"Same." Ryan sits down at a patio table. "I swear I've opened more books in the last week than I have in the last year."

"Maybe it *is* a teacher running the treasure hunt after all," I say. "Maybe this is just a ploy to get students to use the library and open books."

"If that were true, the clue would have been more specific, with a question that required research. Like 'In what year was the Treaty of Guadalupe Hidalgo signed?'"

I blink at him.

"1848, FYI," he says with another charming grin. Ryan's smile should be categorized as a lethal weapon.

I get ahold of myself. "Right. Makes sense. That it's not a teacher." What is wrong with me? I'm entirely capable of speaking in full coherent sentences.

"Where have you checked so far?" Ryan asks, tilting his chair back.

"Everywhere." I wave around the conservatory. "If there aren't any books in here, I have no idea where else to search."

"Maybe the person broke into our rooms? I haven't checked my own books." Ryan puts the chair back firmly onto all four legs.

"That's an idea," I say. But I don't like that thought at all. "Is it that easy to break into our rooms?"

Ryan shrugs. "I mean, there are master keys. The RAs have access to them, but they're only supposed to use them in an emergency."

"Colette can get into the rooms?"

"Technically, yes, but she's the strictest rule follower ever. It's how she got the position. She won't break rules to find rule breakers."

"Then how is it she's even at Last Chance Academy, if she's such a rule follower?" The question just pops out of my mouth.

Ryan doesn't answer. One thing I'm learning is that LCA students keep secrets well. There is no idle gossip. I'm not sure if it's because they feel some kind of loyalty to one another or if it's some unspoken code. Then I recall something Tana said.

"Isn't that how Tana's first roommate got busted? By Colette?" My hands start to feel sweaty, as I think about Colette discovering Sir Grey.

"Yeah." Ryan leans forward, lowering his face to mine where I'm still sitting on the ground. "Colette wasn't the RA, since only eleventh years can be RAs, but she's the one who reported Victoria to Leah, last year's RA. I heard it was contraband and her second offense. No idea what the forbidden item was, though."

Wow. Strict. All the more reason not to trust Colette for sure. "Okay, I'll go check my books. But I really hope the envelopes aren't in dorm rooms."

"Yeah, me too." Ryan stands. "Because that means the ten students who will move on to the next step are already predetermined, and the envelopes aren't all in one book like the original clue said. That wouldn't be fair."

Maybe Ryan hasn't learned that lesson yet. Life isn't fair. Not at all.

CHAPTER 14

LUCK IS WITH ME, and I get back to my room without running into Colette. When Tana returns to our room before dinner, she finds me on the floor looking defeated, with all my books scattered around me. Sir Grey is sitting on the book in front of me.

"You think the envelope is in our room?" Tana asks as she gathers the books on her shelf.

"Not really, but Ryan thought it was a possibility."

That gets Tana to pause and swirl to face me with a smile. "You and Ryan were hanging out?"

I shake my head. "I ran into him. We talked."

Tana sits on her desk chair and spins slowly. "He's so pretty."

"Yeah." I agree. And when Tana keeps grinning at me,

I say, "Don't get any weird ideas." Not only am I not here to make friends but I'm definitely not interested in having crushes.

Tana laughs, not at all offended. "Okay, then."

She hands me a stack of her books, and I shoot her a questioning look. Up till now we haven't really discussed our progress (or lack of) or any ideas surrounding the clue, so it feels strange to go through her books together. But within ten minutes we're finished and we haven't found a silver envelope.

I frown. "You'd think whoever arranged this wouldn't make it so difficult. Do you think anyone else has found an envelope?"

Tana shakes her head. "We would have heard something by now. We're good at keeping things from the administration, but we do talk to one another. It's a very small school."

Our eyes catch as we realize that we're sharing our thoughts, and we both get quiet. We are still competitors, after all.

Sir Grey crawls under my bed while Tana and I clean up our room, putting our books back onto the shelves. It's been almost a week since we got the treasure hunt invitation. Maybe this was all just a cruel joke.

Sir Grey mews. And mews again, but it isn't his usual quiet mew. It sounds like he's in distress. Both Tana and I dive for my bed. She turns on the flashlight that she always carries with her, and there's Sir Grey tangled in the strap of my duffel bag. He squeals pitifully as I drag the bag and him out from under the bed. Tana quickly untangles him. Sir Grey stalks off in a huff and squeezes into my closet, which I leave open a crack.

I look down at my bag. "I guess I should tuck the strap into the bag, so he doesn't get caught again."

When I unzip my bag, Tana looks away. I like that she's not nosy. I'm careful not to peer too closely into the bag. Inside is every single treasure Mom ever gave me, and my collection of origami projects. I didn't want to leave them behind, but I'm also not ready to look at them. My hand skims the silver envelope, which I shoved into the bag after I received it. I pull it out before sliding my bag back under the bed.

I read over the invitation again, slowly. My eyes snag on the last line, and I read it out loud, "Small print: good luck."

Tana now peers over my shoulder. "What about it?" she asks.

Mom's treasure hunt clues were never straightforward. They were riddles or puzzles. Although, to be fair, they were usually pretty easy to solve. I glance at Tana. I could blow off her question, but we were just now talking about the clue. Plus, my mind is busy spinning with ideas to solve this problem.

So I read the entire invitation out loud. "You are cordially invited to play, and win an all-expenses-paid luxury vacation to Newport Beach, California, over winter break. You choose your chaperone. There are only three rules: One, for the entirety of the game, no matter if you are playing or eliminated, if any administrator, staff, RA, or twelfth-year student discovers what you're up to, the game is off. Don't ruin it for others. Two, there are ten silver envelopes hidden in a book. Take only one. Ten participants will move on to the next round. Three, have fun." I tap my finger on the last line and read it again. "Small print: good luck."

Tana remains quiet and still, but her breathing gets faster, like she's waiting and anticipating.

I get so excited by that brain-humming feeling that comes with figuring out a puzzle that I don't give Tana a second thought. My eyes skim the last line. *Small print: good luck.* Everything in the invitation is straightforward. Just telling us that the envelopes are in a book is not very helpful. It's too general. It could take forever to go through every book in the school. What if this last line is actually a clue? An idea comes to me. I hate to give away even the slightest of clues, but Tana is the fastest way to get the answer. I need to be one of the ten players.

I turn to Tana. "Is there another library in the school? Like, smaller than the one the students use?"

"There is!" Tana's eyes are bright. "The staff library!"

Voices come from the hall as girls pass our door. I lower my voice. "Where is the staff library? Is it much smaller?" The words "small print" could definitely refer to a smaller library. Maybe.

"I have no idea. No students are allowed there. I just know about it because Leah, last year's RA, mentioned it when she had to deliver a note to a teacher in the staff library."

"Do you know where it is?" I'm getting excited, but my excitement deflates when Tana shakes her head.

"I can ask Leah," she offers.

"No way. She's a twelfth year. Don't forget the rules."

"Oh yeah." Tana frowns.

I count in my head. "There are, what, six twelfth years?"

Tana nods.

"That leaves twenty-nine students. Minus the two current RAs, at the most there are twenty-seven of us playing. If you breathe a word about the staff library, someone else will figure it out. There are ten envelopes. Let's get the first two!"

Tana bobs her head so hard, her curls bounce. "Yes!"

I dig through my desk drawer and bring out the map Dr. Ward handed me that first day. I spread it out on the floor in front of me and Tana. I trace a finger along all the places I know and have been through, except the boys' wing, which is off-limits.

"What's over here?" I tap to the right of the map, off the paper.

"Our rug?" Tana says, wrinkling her nose in confusion.

I smile. "No, I mean there has to be a whole section that's not on the map. The foyer is the center of the building, and everything on this map—our dorms, the classrooms—is off to the left."

"You're right!"

"We need to get over to the staff and administration side," I say. Ms. Sheth told us that some of the teachers and staff, like her, live at LCA since the school is so isolated.

"You're in?" I ask Tana. I'm not much for teaming up, but it's too late now. Besides, there are ten envelopes. It can't hurt to work with her for now. I'll work alone for the next part.

"Yes," she says, "but I think we need one more person."

"What? No."

Tana nods. "Even if we find the staff library, I guarantee it will be locked tight."

"Okay. Then, who do you want to have join us?"

"Zane Yoshikawa."

"No way," I say. I don't trust him at all. He's surly and quiet. Too quiet. The kind of quiet that means he's taking everything in and giving away nothing. "Why Zane?"

"Because he can break in anywhere."

CHAPTER 15

"ZANE'S PARENTS WERE KILLED in a car accident when he was eight," Tana explains. "He went to live with a family friend. But that family friend taught Zane how to pick pockets and break into houses and shops. Apparently he was very good. When he got caught, it came out that his guardian was responsible for a bunch of burglaries. An anonymous patron gave Zane a scholarship, and that's why he's here."

"How do you know all this?" I've found it impossible to learn why each student is at Last Chance Academy. It doesn't seem like the kind of thing you outright ask someone. Tana hasn't asked me why I'm here, and I haven't asked her.

Tana shrugs. "Jung Song is good at getting not only supplies but also information."

"You paid to find that out?"

"No. Zane started in the middle of sixth year, and my former roomie was nosy, rich, and not very good at keeping secrets. She got the info, and then she blabbered to me one night. I haven't told anyone else, though."

I sigh. I don't like having to bring a third person into this, but Tana is probably right. We won't be able to break into that library. And if my plan is to work, we will only have one shot at this. It's too late to back out of sharing with Tana, and none of this matters if we can't get those envelopes.

"Okay," I say. "Here's the plan."

"Wait," she says. "I want to be honest. I'm teaming with you for now. Once we get the next clue, we will be competitors. I mean, we're still friends and all, but also, I intend to win."

She called us friends. I harden the look on my face. "Fair. And just so you know, I'm going to win."

"We'll see," Tana says with a grin. "Also, I promise, you can trust me. I won't betray you or stab you in the back to win. I always win honestly."

I don't know about trusting her. I mean, I don't trust anyone anymore, but for now I'll have to.

"It has to be Saturday night," I explain. "With the Saturday evening activity being outdoors, it will be harder to keep track of us. I heard that Colette won't be with us because she has some meeting with a teacher. And I have my Saturday evening phone call with my dad, so I get to leave dinner early."

Last week Dr. Ward escorted me to the phone but disappeared into her office during my too-short call. I knocked on her door when I was done, but when she opened it and saw me there, she looked annoyed and told me I could just join evening activities without disturbing her. So this time I can just leave and go straight to the staff side of the manor, knowing Dr. Ward will be holed up in her office. I explain to Tana, and her eyes grow wide.

"You're just going to wander around? How will you find the library?"

"*We* will find it," I say, confident.

"We?" Tana sounds less confident, less bubbly. Less Tana. "No way. I can't afford to get busted. I love the computer programming I'm learning here. I don't want to get expelled."

"None of us want to get caught," I say. I've got to get Tana on board. I'm not going to be the only one taking a risk here after giving away a clue.

"How are Zane and I going to get away?" Tana asks.

"Right after dinner, when everyone goes back to their rooms to change for the evening activity, you both head over to me," I say. Not every student changes out of their uniform, but most of us are happy to wear regular clothes when we're given permission.

"How about only Zane joins you?" Tana says. "It'll be more suspicious if two of us are missing. I can run interference."

I shake my head. "The rules say we can each take one envelope."

"How will they know?"

"Do you want to take the chance that the extra envelope Zane and I get for you will count? It's your choice."

Tana frowns. "Fine. But you talk to Zane."

"What? Me? Why?"

"You're the only one he's ever spoken to voluntarily. At least in public."

"Really?"

"He has never, ever talked to us in class or at mealtimes. Ever, except to you," Tana says with a shrug.

Great. So now I have to be the one to somehow convince him to join us on Saturday. Zane doesn't strike me as a joiner. This is going to be a challenge.

CHAPTER 16

I DON'T GET A chance to talk to Zane at dinner. There's no privacy at all. I have to find a way to get him alone, something I haven't needed or wanted to do till now.

If I thought talking privately was hard during the regular class days, it's impossible on Friday. During test prep in the morning, it's completely silent. I glance at Ms. Sheth, who is busy grading papers at the front of the room, allowing us to study in peace.

I have my first official test in an hour in social studies, and I don't want to mess up. It's one thing if Colette gets me in trouble. Obviously, I can't really control that, but I can control my grades. When Mom was around, I was an excellent student. And an even better treasure hunter. Priorities.

Immediately after we hand in our social studies test, Tana turns to us. "How do you think you did?"

"I think I did okay," I say, relieved. I was able to answer each question without hesitation.

Tana studies me. "But do you think you got one hundred percent?"

"How do I know?"

Ryan laughs and explains, "Tana has to get the highest score. Always. And she always has. She's trying to figure out what kind of competition she has in you."

"Oh." I smile sweetly at her. "I think you definitely have competition now."

She fake pouts. "We'll see." Tana goes up to Ms. Maynor's desk and stands there patiently. The benefit (or drawback, depending on how you feel) of having such a small class is that most of the time you get your grades immediately after taking your exam.

Ms. Maynor has been teaching at LCA for several years, and she knows Tana and her drive for success.

Ryan tilts his chair back. "I'm glad we're done with the exam. And we get to be outdoors tomorrow night! Fresh air, space, stretching out!"

To no one's surprise, Zane puts his head down on the desk and disengages, leaving me to talk with Ryan. "Yep," I say. "The great outdoors!"

I don't owe Ryan anything, and this treasure hunt is

a competition, but I wonder if Zane will tell Ryan once I invite him to join us? I glance at Tana, who continues to hover over Ms. Maynor. I definitely wouldn't tell Tana if someone gave me a hint. There will only be one winner, and that winner is going to be me.

Ms. Maynor finally puts her pen down and smiles at Tana. "Just barely, Ms. Rabin, but you beat Ms. Mizuno by two points."

Tana raises her hands in triumph, but I detect a worried glint in her eyes. I only care about staying enrolled, but now that Tana has made this a competition, maybe I will study harder.

At lunch I refocus my attention on Zane and ponder my options. He's quiet and private, but because of my excellent observation skills, I've figured out a few things about him. During independent study he doesn't meet with any of the usual teachers or staff. It's someone else who comes for Zane, a scruffy white dude who dresses like he's about to go on safari. I'm still trying to figure out what Zane's study is. I'm confident I'll know by next week. Plus, by then I'll need to be on my own independent study, and I'll lose my wandering privileges.

Friday after lunch is extracurricular time. We aren't with our year, so I won't see him. It's LCA's way of making the different years interact with one another like in gym. But I can follow Zane and try to catch him. For the next four weeks I have art. The instructor, Santiago Mariscal, is a professional artist with paintings in galleries. He doesn't take attendance but expects us to show him our progress at the end of the hour. So even if I'm late, as long as I have something to show him, I'll be fine.

After we finish eating, I head out of the dining room to follow Zane. If anything, I'm stealthy.

Or maybe not.

When I turn the corner, I nearly run into Zane. He's leaning against the wall, arms crossed, with his usual scowl. Like he's waiting. I yelp.

"Are you looking for me?" he asks, his voice low.

I want to play it cool. In my head I look totally innocent. But the corner of Zane's mouth twitches, and he surprises me a second time.

"Are you actually smirking?" I ask.

His mouth returns to a straight line. "You're stalking me, Mizuno."

"I'm not, Yoshikawa."

A few seconds pass, and neither of us makes a move. But he has the upper hand. I do need something from him. And it bugs me that he knows it.

"I'm going to be late to music." He says this like he doesn't care either way, but I'm pretty sure he, like me, and probably like most of the students, doesn't want to lose a spot here at LCA.

"Fine. I think I know where the envelopes are hidden."

He raises an eyebrow. "And you're telling me because?"

"You don't want to know?"

"Maybe I already have an envelope."

"Do you?" I ask without remembering to act like I hold all the cards. When he doesn't answer, I sigh. "If you want to join me and Tana, meet me by the staff restroom near the main foyer after dinner tomorrow."

"Why are you telling me any of this?"

The chime sounds, signaling the start of the next period. We are now late to extracurricular.

"Don't tell anyone. Come ready to pick a lock," I say as I move past him, not giving him a chance to respond.

I have a strong feeling he'll show up.

CHAPTER 17

WHEN I GET TO Dr. Ward's sitting room on Saturday evening, as soon as I sit down on the leather chair, the land-line rings. Dad is never late, at least.

"Megumi." Dad's voice comes through the earpiece and warms me like a hug. I want to go home.

"Hi, Dad," I say. "How's work?"

I don't really care much about his job, but that always gets him talking. As he rambles on about deals and travel-ing, I watch the time. Of course he's chatty tonight. I need to get moving.

When he pauses for a breath, I tell him we have an astronomy activity.

"Is astronomy something you're interested in?" he asks.

"Kind of?" I have no opinion on this except, like I said,

I'm not much of an outdoor person. The most outdoorsy I ever got was for Mom's treasure hunts.

I glance at Dr. Ward's closed office door. There will be other Saturdays and other phone calls with Dad. There will not be other opportunities to get those envelopes.

"I'll talk to you next week?" I ask.

"Just a minute," he says. "I need to talk to you about something."

This doesn't sound good.

"As you know, I'm traveling a lot. I'm hardly home. And with you away at Leland Chase Academy, the house is pretty much empty all the time."

I'm strangling the phone against my ear as if it might make Dad stop talking.

"It doesn't make sense to keep the house," Dad continues. "I'm putting it on the market."

It's hard for me to breathe. I can't even get any words out.

"Megumi?"

Finally the dam bursts and I release a flood of questions. "When? When are you selling the house? And where are you going to live? Are you never coming home again? What about me? Do I not have a home anymore?"

"Megumi, slow down," Dad says. "I won't put the house on the market until early next year. We need to prepare the house for listing. When you come home for winter break, we'll pack up the house. Together."

He says this like he thinks it's supposed to be a special treat for us.

"And," he continues, clueless that he's shattering my heart, "Aunt Vivian has generously opened her home to us. She has more than enough room."

"You're moving in with Aunt Vivian?" I choke on the words.

"Well, more like staying with her when I'm not traveling," Dad says, his voice breaking a little. "It might be nice, Megumi, for us to have Aunt Vivian around."

When I don't say anything, he continues. "It makes sense this way. You already have a room there, and we can move the rest of your things. This will be our new home, Megumi."

It will never be home. Dad wants to leave the one place that has all of Mom in it, our things, our traditions. He wants to abandon our memories of her. I won't let him.

I need to win the prize to Newport Beach. I will spend that time with him reminding him that we're a family and we don't need Aunt Vivian. I will convince him not to sell our home, because that's all we have left of Mom.

I'm angry at myself for bringing Tana and Zane into getting the first envelopes. It's too late now. With ten envelopes, there will be another clue, and this time I won't be working with anyone else. I need to cut them loose as soon as possible.

"I have to go, Dad." I hang up quietly before he can say anything else.

CHAPTER 18

I SILENTLY LEAVE Dr. Ward's office suite, chanting my objective in my head. *Get the envelope. Dump Tana and Zane. Win at all costs.* I wish I didn't need Tana or Zane, but the cold, hard truth is that I needed Tana to learn about the staff library and we need Zane to break in. One step at a time.

No one else is around, and I easily make it down a dark hall to the archway leading to the staff restroom. I tuck myself behind the outcropping of the arch and wait.

My heart pounds when I hear soft footfalls. I'm relieved to see Zane and Tana. I try not to look too triumphant when Zane catches my eyes. He responds with an eye roll.

I put my finger to my lips (these walls echo) and start down the dimly lit hall. I'm guessing that the layout is similar on both sides, and so far I'm correct. I find a flight of stairs and climb it. I assume the staff library will be out of reach to the students but not inaccessible, since teachers and staff use it. Second floor, I think.

When we get to the landing, Tana's breathing is a bit heavier. Zane is so stealthy that I think he's abandoned us, but when I stop, he's still here with us.

Tana's hands are clenched into tight fists. She's stressed. Zane, however, looks like he's out for a stroll. But while his shoulders are relaxed, I can tell he's on high alert by the way he keeps cocking his head as if he's listening. My heart skips, and I recognize that it's not fear or worry but excitement. The same feeling I used to get on my treasure hunts with Mom.

We walk down the hall, and I'm right. These rooms look like offices, with different teacher and staff names on doors. I make a couple of wrong turns (okay, more than a couple), but neither Tana nor Zane comment. It's weird how quiet and empty this floor is, but I suspect that the living quarters are on the third floor.

Finally! We get to a door marked STAFF LIBRARY. I press my ear to it and hear nothing, but these doors are very thick. There's no guarantee that this room is empty. I slowly turn the doorknob. As expected, locked. I notice that the doors on the staff side of the manor have modern locks, while our dorm rooms have old-fashioned, simple keyhole locks.

Without a word Zane steps forward, and Tana and I fall back. Good thing Tana's so nervous about getting caught that her eyes are on the hallway. I can watch Zane.

Zane kneels in front of the door and pulls out a small zippered case. When he leans forward, his hair falls into his eyes in soft waves. He opens the case. His hands are steady and his fingers are slim, like he could play the piano. Inside the case is a bunch of silver picks in different shapes.

"Is that a lock-picking kit?" I whisper.

He nods as he pulls out a thin L-shaped pick.

"But how did you get that through inspection when you moved here? All my bags were checked," I say.

He shoots me a glare. "Do you want me to do this or not?"

"Stop talking, both of you," Tana whispers. "You're going to get us caught."

Zane pulls out another pick that has a squigglier end, and says, "Jung Song."

"But I thought she didn't get things that were illegal," I say, keeping my voice low.

"Lock picks are not illegal," he says as he slides the L-shaped one into the lock with the handle straight up.

I'm about to say something else, but Tana jabs me, hard, in the side. I get the hint and shut up. Zane sticks in the other pick, jiggling it gingerly, and a few seconds later the L-shaped one turns, and the door opens!

Zane puts his tools away, and I catch the satisfied smile on his face. The first real smile I've seen on him. He steps back quietly, but by now Tana is breathing so hard that anyone close by might hear. I raise my finger to my lips. She gives me a helpless shrug and tries to quiet her breathing.

I listen at the crack of the open door. Nothing. But then again it is a library. Ready to act like I got lost, I push the door all the way open.

The room is dark. And empty.

It's a small room, cozy, with dark red papered walls and a low ceiling painted in cream with gold accents. Bookcases line the walls, and in the center of the room, on Persian rugs, are comfortable-looking chairs and sofas. Perfect for curling up with a good book.

No words are needed. After I shut and lock the door, I turn on the light and we split up. Fortunately, this library is much smaller than the student one, and we make quick work of it. I'm starting to think I was wrong about the clue when I hear Zane whisper, "Found them."

Tana and I scurry over to him. There in a thick leather book titled *Secrets of English Manors* is a stack of silver envelopes. Ten of them. We are first! Quickly we each take one. I shove mine into the back of my waistband, covering it with my cardigan, and Tana and Zane follow suit. Zane replaces the book, and we escape out of the library and back to the foyer without getting caught.

It's hard not to let the grin take over my face. I feel giddy. I even take a second to exchange smiles with Tana and Zane, who look equally triumphant.

So as not to be obvious, we take turns joining the ongoing activity outside, and nobody notices.

Or so I think.

CHAPTER 19

IT TAKES EVERY BIT of patience in me (which, to be honest, is not a lot) to keep from finding a hiding spot to open the envelope. It looks like we missed the nature hike, I notice as I join the group looking up at the constellations. Dr. Chen drones on in a pleasant voice. Like a lullaby. I'm jolted out of the peaceful feeling when Ryan sidles up to me.

"Where were you, Zane, and Tana?" he whispers into my ear, sending a shiver down my back.

"I don't know what you're talking about," I whisper back.

He makes a sound, and when I turn to him, I'm surprised to see a hurt look on his face. Not that I care. But there *are* seven more envelopes. And it would be smart to be able to keep my eye on the competition.

"Did you know that there's a small staff library on the other side of the manor?" I ask, and then I slide away from him.

Back in our room Tana and I wait till after room check before we open the envelopes. We sit side by side on the floor between our beds. Sir Grey has gotten used to the routine and remains in my closet until lights-out.

"Ready?" Tana asks, her excitement finally overtaking her nerves.

I nod. At the same time we open our envelopes. Inside are silver sun stickers. We pull out the stickers and cards that look exactly like the first notes, but with different instructions, and this time they're signed.

> Congratulations!
> You are moving on to the next round.
> Place the enclosed sticker on the bottom of
> the window on your side of the room (to
> distinguish from your roommate's side).
> Await the next envelope.
> Do not get caught.
> ~The Mastermind

The stickers peel off from the backing so that they are face-out on the glass. We manage to place them on our windows just before lights-out. I climb into bed, and Sir Grey curls up next to my head as always.

"The Mastermind," Tana says softly. "Sounds sinister, doesn't it?"

I shrug even though I know she can't see me.

"Good night, Meg," Tana says as she always does.

And while I have never answered her, in my head I say, *Game on.*

CHAPTER 20

I TAKE ADVANTAGE OF my last week of freedom during independent study and lurk outdoors, checking windows. Either Ryan blabbed or students caught on, because by Wednesday, I count ten silver suns in windows. As I find the tenth sun in a window, I run into Zane, who has a camera around his neck.

"Hey," I say.

Zane nods and walks past me into the gardens. What a snob! He can't even say hello after Tana and I led him to an envelope? He never even thanked me or said another word. At least Ryan said thanks first thing in Life Skills on Monday morning.

Of course, then I had to explain to Tana what I'd done and had to suffer her knowing look. She thought I'd done it because I have a crush. That's not it at all. I just like to know who my competition is.

She's gone silent about the treasure hunt, but that's fine. If I win—when I win—I'll get Dad to take a vacation and we'll go to California together. We haven't been on vacation since Mom died. Not that I expected us to. It seems like Dad's way of coping is cutting himself off. I truly get it, because I don't want to spend time with anyone else. But I would like to spend time with Dad. When I win and we go on this vacation, it will remind Dad that we're family. It will make Dad want to settle back home with me.

On my way to study hall, I run into Miss Jillian. From what I've observed, there's a rotating group of five security staff. Mrs. Jackson is head of security and a little scary. Miss Jillian seems to be the friendliest, but Tana says she's new.

"Do you have a pass?" she asks, holding her hand out.

I hand over the now crumpled note from my cardigan pocket.

Miss Jillian skims it and hands it back to me. "Dr. Ward wants to see you," she says.

Now what? My heart hammers as I consider the possibility that Dr. Ward is onto the treasure hunt or at least suspects something.

Miss Jillian walks me into Dr. Ward's office and disappears. I sit and wait as Dr. Ward finishes writing something in a big notebook. I try not to be too obvious, but it looks like one of those old-fashioned accounting things that I once saw Ojiichan, my grandpa, writing in, when he ran a little shop near our house. I used to love hanging out with him when I was little. He died when I was five. Come to think of it, that's when Mom started the treasure hunts.

Dr. Ward closes the notebook and leans back, finally looking at me with her stern gaze.

"You have had ample time," Dr. Ward starts, with no greeting of any kind. No checking in about how my first couple of weeks at LCA have been going. "What is your intended independent study?"

"I thought I had till Friday?" I squeak.

"If you don't know it now, you won't know it Friday. Are you telling me you haven't decided?"

I think quickly, because no, I haven't decided. I'm pretty sure "treasure hunter" isn't an acceptable IS topic. But I have loved the freedom I've had these last couple of weeks.

Fortunately, Miss Annie, Dr. Ward's administrative assistant, knocks and interrupts us, saying that there's a problem. Dr. Ward instructs me to stay put, and she leaves the office. I use the time wisely to ponder. Zane was wandering around while I was. I suspect his independent study is photography. (Okay, it doesn't take an observant genius to have figured that out.) I do not want to be with him doing the same thing, but I want to pick something that allows me that same kind of freedom. Living here at LCA, with all the rules and schedules and Colette hovering, has made me feel claustrophobic.

Dr. Ward bustles back in and asks, "Megumi, what is your independent study?"

"Nature," I say, hoping I haven't made a bad choice.

Dr. Ward scribbles in a different ledger. Wow. She's really old-school. "Fine. We already have Carole Rogers on payroll, so she will be your sponsor. I'll make arrangements and let you know when to meet her. In the meantime you'll have extra study time in Ms. Sheth's room."

No more wandering around alone. I sit there for a beat, not sure if I've been dismissed. Dr. Ward opens the first ledger again, and I stand up to leave. There are a lot of numbers that are in dollars, and they are getting smaller.

When Dr. Ward looks up at me, I quickly leave the room, wondering what those numbers mean.

CHAPTER 21

THE NEXT ENVELOPES COME after lights-out. For that reason alone the person running the treasure hunt has to be someone on campus. Also, how else would they know that all ten sun stickers are in place?

Tana and I creep to the door and pick up our envelopes. We return to our beds. I open the envelope carefully in case there's something else in it like another sticker, but this time it's just the card. There's a full moon and enough light to read by.

Megumi Mizuno,
There are ten items hidden together somewhere inside the manor. Find and collect the one meant for you and display it in your window. Do not

take anyone else's. The first five to display their
items will move on and get another envelope.
Your clue: using your best language is key.
Your item: your mom.
Good luck!
~The Mastermind

My heart lodges in my throat when I read the words "your mom." It's shocking and disturbing. What is this Mastermind up to? And how do they know anything about me? I haven't told anyone here about Mom.

I had zero intention of discussing this with Tana, but I'm too surprised. I hop over to her bed and sit on the edge.

"Is your hint specifically for you?" I whisper.

Tana doesn't answer. I'm disappointed, but I get it. We are competitors. But when I glance at her, the look on her face isn't her usual fierce look but rather . . . fear?

"Tana?" I reach out and gently nudge her. "Are you okay?"

She still doesn't move. She's gripping her card so tightly that it's bent. I reach over and pause. Tana doesn't react. I slowly slip it out of her grip and lean toward the window so I can read it. It starts out the same.

Tana Rabin,
There are ten items hidden together somewhere
inside the manor. Find and collect the one meant

for you and display it in your window. Do not take anyone else's. The first five to display their items will move on and get another envelope. Your clue: using your best language is key. Your item: your aunt. Good luck! ~The Mastermind

"Well, at least this time we know that there's a clue," I say.

Tana's frozen posture worries me. Her eyes remain focused on the space where her card was in her hands moments ago.

"I mean, it's pretty vague. Also, what is this item we're looking for supposed to be?" I curse to myself in Japanese. I'm doing the thing I said I wouldn't do. Care. But I also don't like that Tana is obviously upset.

"Tana?" I shake her gently. "Tana!"

She finally hears me. She blinks and then stares at her empty hands. I give her back her clue card. And to be fair, I show her mine. She reads it, and in the moonlight I see the color come back into her cheeks.

She takes a breath, and then another deeper one. "I guess something about your mom is private? Something you haven't told anyone, or a lot of people?" she asks.

I nod. "She died of an aneurysm when I was in the fifth

grade," I say with as little emotion as possible. And that is all I'm going to say on that. To Tana's credit she doesn't press.

Suddenly a shout comes from one of the other rooms on our hall.

We both scramble to the door. I open it but see nothing, then quickly shut it when I hear a door open and Colette's voice ringing down the hall. "What is going on?"

Tana and I freeze as we hear her footfalls approach and pass our door. I open the door a crack so we can listen. Colette has homed in on the offending room. Her sharp knock echoes. I try to think who is in the last room. I don't have to guess, because I hear Colette identify them.

"Paisley Schoenholz and Zarifa Haddad, one demerit each for making noise after lights-out," Colette says loudly, and definitely on purpose. I'll bet every one of us has our door cracked to eavesdrop. It's unfair because it's not as if they were having a party or a loud conversation. It was one shout. A warning would have been fair. But Colette is anything but fair.

Paisley and Zarifa are both tenth years. I quietly close our door before Colette returns. Tana and I wait until we hear the RA pass our room again.

I return to my bed. Tana follows me and perches at the foot. Sir Grey silently slinks out of my closet and leaps onto Tana's lap, sensing she needs comfort.

"Either Paisley or Zarifa got an envelope," I say, mostly to myself. From outside I saw three stickers on this side of the girls' wing. Mine, Tana's, and now I know, Paisley and Zarifa's room. On the other side, I counted one sticker, and it wasn't Jung Song's room. I finally figured out where the boys' wing windows are, and I counted six stickers. Zane and Ryan's room was the only window with two stickers.

"Probably something on the clue card shocked them," Tana says. She leans her head back against my wall. "My aunt runs her own online business."

"Oh. Cool." But I know there's more, so I wait.

Tana looks at me, and in the moonlight her eyes are luminous, like they could pull me in.

"I'm a hacker," she says.

"**MY PARENTS ENROLLED ME** at LCA because of
the restrictions on personal electronic devices and because
they monitor computer use," Tana continues. "I'm here
because I broke into my middle school's computer system.
It was the summer before I was going to start there. I wasn't
going to do anything bad. I just wanted to see if I could."

"But you got caught," I say.

She nods, her curls bouncing. "I got caught. That time."

"*That* time?"

Tana shrugs, but she doesn't go on. Which means she
didn't get caught some other time. To try to make her reveal
more, I share a little of my story.

"It was a shock when my mom died," I say, letting the
words tumble out fast, because if I let myself think too hard

about it, I'll fall apart. "I couldn't remember a time when she'd ever been sick, not even with a cold. She was healthier than anyone else I knew. She ran all the time, loved to go hiking, and was always taking some kind of class with a friend. She volunteered at an animal shelter three times a week.

"That's where she was when she died. It was instant, they say."

Tana makes a sound like she's about to speak. I cut her off because nothing she says will bring my mom back. Nothing she says will make it better.

"I stopped caring about anything, after that," I say. "Including school. Dad sent me to live with my horrible aunt. I started to cut school. I didn't do my assignments or take tests. I was flunking out of sixth grade, and I didn't care. And then Dad found Leland Chase Academy, and here I am. If I get kicked out of here, he's sending me back to my aunt's to be homeschooled."

Tana nods and says, "I was in the third grade when I broke into my mom's phone. I guessed her passcode. She thought it was cute. That was my first taste of hacking. I started playing around on the home computer, breaking into my parents' different online accounts for fun. In fifth grade I got serious. My first real success at hacking anyone outside of my house was my aunt's company. But I wasn't careful, and I left a door open, and she got hacked by someone else and it cost her a lot of money. I knew it was my fault, but I never said anything."

"But someone knows," I say, nodding at her card.

"The Mastermind," Tana says.

"But how?" I ask. "And why?"

Tana physically shakes herself off, startling Sir Grey. He flicks his tail at her and moves over to me.

"You know what?" Tana says. "It doesn't matter. All that matters is the final prize. Winning." She smiles at me. "I'm going to win."

"We'll see."

I feel a glimmer of something unfamiliar. Joy? Anticipation? After having a little heart-to-heart with Tana, even though I did it purposely to find out more about her background, I feel like something has changed in a good way between us.

Then I come to my senses and put my good feelings in check. No friendships, no attachments. I'm not staying, and I'm not getting hurt again.

But that doesn't mean I need to make an enemy of my roommate. Sharing a room and all. It's better to get along.

CHAPTER 23

ON THURSDAY, ONCE AGAIN there's no real opportunity to discuss anything with anyone else during class time. And none of us is taking a chance anymore by talking about it during mealtimes. But I catch the furtive glances and nods as classmates pass one another or sit down in the dining hall.

I'm heading to Ms. Sheth's, where I'll be stuck until Carole Rogers is available for my first official independent study meeting. I walk slowly, peering around corners, looking for hidden nooks, hoping to find my item. I spent half the night thinking about the clue—best language. Maybe we talk to someone, and they'll hand us the item? Using our best language could be that we have to be polite? Only the older students take foreign languages. Could that be part of the clue? But I still don't feel like I've hit on what the clue means.

There is nothing in the rules saying we can't help one another, only that we can't let any outsiders discover the treasure hunt. Not that I'm going to team up, but it seems unfair if others are getting help.

From what I can see, this is a fun game to the other students. It doesn't look like anyone else is taking it too seriously. Or maybe they're just good at hiding their intentions. I mean, from what I understand, everyone is here for a reason. They got into trouble or got kicked out of school. Then again, these students come from very wealthy families, and a luxury vacation isn't out of their reach.

But Tana, she has that drive to win. And I want to win for my mom and to get Dad to go on vacation with me so I can convince him to keep our home. If anything, the real competition is between Tana and me.

I wish my item were more specific. "Your mom" can mean a lot of things. It's possible my item is more random. Like a MOM sticker or something.

This is hurting my head.

"What's with the frown?" Ryan suddenly appears, his usual bright, open smile on his very pretty face.

"Hey," I say. I glance around the hall and see no one else, but I lower my voice anyway. "You and Zane got envelopes?"

Ryan nods, his hair flopping a bit. It's adorable. *Focus, Megumi!*

"And?" I ask.

"Ah, ah," Ryan says with a teasing lilt. "Nothing is free. What did yours say?"

I shrug. "Like you said, nothing is free. Tell me yours first."

"What are you two doing here?"

We both jump as Colette barrels toward us. Her eyes look like fire, and her mouth is moving like she's chewing something bitter. Her hands are clenched, and as she gets closer, my stomach flips. This is it. She's going to give me fifty demerits and I'll be kicked out of the school. My whole life does not flash before my eyes, but instead my bleak future plays out, where I'm stuck at Aunt Vivian's being homeschooled by her. I groan quietly.

Ryan nudges me, and when I look up at him, he winks!

"I asked you both a question," Colette says as she stops in front of us.

"Oh, hi, Colette," Ryan says in a honeyed voice I haven't heard before. "Good to see you. How's your project coming along?"

I don't expect Colette to be distracted, even though Ryan's voice is super smooth. I'm surprised when her scowl drops and her mouth curves into a real smile. It's a little unsettling, actually. She looks like a completely different person.

"It's good," she says in a chipper voice. "Thanks for the suggestion. Totally did the trick."

Ryan nods. "That's great! We were just heading to independent study, but I had a question for Meg about our essay. You know me, sometimes I have a hard time paying attention."

The way he says "You know me" sounds like he and she share something. She nods knowingly. I watch open-mouthed. It's incredible, the effect he has on her, even though she's, like, four years older than he is. It's not in a creepy way but more like she's charmed by him, taken in by him. Like an older sister would be. This is almost as fascinating as when Zane was picking the lock.

Colette sighs. "Well, okay, but you need to get going or you'll be late. I don't want to hand out demerits."

What? I'm pretty sure Colette lives to hand out demerits.

Ryan turns to me and nods. "Let's go, Meg." He waves me in front of him, and I see what he's doing. If he leaves me behind, Colette will surely turn on me. But she's still under his spell of sorts, and off we go.

"That was scary amazing," I say once we are out of her sight.

Ryan grins at me, making my heart skip a beat. "You're welcome. You owe me." And he turns the corner heading to wherever he goes for independent study.

CHAPTER 24

SATURDAY MORNING, MY ALARM goes off at six, waking Tana, too. Sir Grey mews at the rude awakening and stalks to my closet.

"Meg? What the heck?" Tana sits up, her hair poofed out like a lion's mane. "It's too early even for me."

It *is* too early, but if I want to find my item, I need to take advantage of having an entire morning to myself. As far as I know, no one else has found theirs yet. When I get dressed, Tana grumbles.

"I know what you're up to, Meg," she says, looking under her bed for her socks. "I was going to do the same, but not so early."

I grin. "You can go back to bed."

We both know that's not going to happen. I'm ready

first. I grab Sir Grey's litter box trash and shove it into my bag.

"You're going to have to meet up with Jung again soon," Tana says. "We're almost out of cat food."

I noticed that last night. "I'll make a stop later." I'm pretty sure Jung isn't up yet, and I also know she isn't playing. Maybe she isn't into treasure hunts. Supplying students probably keeps her plenty busy, and it's lucrative. She doesn't strike me as a California-beach-vacation type anyway.

After I dump the kitty trash, I stop at the back door of the kitchen. It's quiet. Very quiet. Nobody is up yet. Optional breakfast is at nine, two hours later than during the week, so not even the kitchen staff is around. Which makes it the perfect time to check it out, one of the few places I haven't been to on the student side of the manor.

I try the door and it's unlocked. So maybe someone is here. But when I step in, the kitchen is empty and silent. And clean. Super clean. I open drawers and cabinets, but I know the items won't be somewhere so obvious. I move through the kitchen into the pantry. Again, it seems an unlikely place to hide something. I'm about to leave when I hear the kitchen door click open.

I spin around in the pantry, but there's nowhere to hide. I tuck myself next to the doorway, hoping that if someone walks in, I can duck out before they spot me.

I strain to hear footsteps but hear nothing. Pressing back against the shelf, trying to make myself small, I forget I have my backpack on. I hit a couple of bottles and they clink. I freeze. Holding my breath, I close my eyes, like that might make me invisible.

So even when I hear someone step into the pantry, and even when I feel a waft of air in front of my face, I keep my eyes shut tight, until I hear, "Found you," and my eyes fly open.

CHAPTER 25

I RECOGNIZE THE VOICE immediately.

"What are you doing here?" I ask Zane. He's in uniform too, as required, but his tie is loose, and the top button of his shirt is undone. We're not allowed to wear jewelry of any kind other than an analog watch, but I catch a glimpse of silver around his neck.

"The same thing you're doing." Zane takes a quick look around the pantry and steps back out.

I don't follow him. I'll wait till he's gone before I continue my search. I hear him moving things around, opening drawers. I shake my head. Again, there's no way the Mastermind hid things in such an obvious place, where people look all the time.

I drop my backpack to the floor and peer at the cans

on a shelf. Something glints in the far back corner. I move a few cans over to get a better look. There is a small space between the boards of the shelf. I have to stand on my toes and nearly climb onto the shelf, but in the narrow opening is a switch of some sort. One of those metal toggle things. I stretch, and my finger barely fits into the space. With the tip of my finger, I flick the switch, and I hear a very distinct click.

"What did you find?" Zane's voice comes from behind me.

I swear he's like Sir Grey, so quiet on his feet. Instead of answering him I go ahead and give the shelf a nudge. Waiting longer for Zane to leave would mean possibly bumping into the kitchen staff. The whole wall moves slightly, making a space just big enough for me to squeeze through.

"Holy . . . ," Zane breathes. "Is this a secret door?"

That means he hasn't found any other hidden rooms. I smile to myself even though I've given this one away. I step into the narrow opening and am not surprised when Zane follows. There is barely enough room to walk, and even so, I have to turn sideways to continue farther along the path. It's then that I hear voices. Zane and I freeze as the voices get louder. It's the kitchen staff, here for breakfast prep.

"The door," I say softly.

Zane slithers silently, smoothly to the shelf and pushes it closed with a click. And then I remember. My backpack.

But it's too late, we can hear a voice as someone steps into the pantry. "Why are the cans all messed up?"

The cans scrape as the person arranges them back into order.

"Hey." The same voice comes again. "Did any of you leave a backpack here last night?"

I hold in a groan as Zane shoots me an annoyed look. I admit it. That was extremely careless of me.

"It looks like a student's," says another voice. "Maybe whoever was helping yesterday?"

"I'll take it to lost and found," says the first voice.

I'm relieved. I'll pick it up later.

Nothing I can do about it now, and we're not going to be able to leave through that opening for the rest of the day, since the kitchen will be occupied. I start scooting along the pathway, but my hand hits the wall. The sound is minuscule, and with all the racket the staff is now making, it's unlikely they heard, but Zane hisses at me.

"Be careful," he scolds quietly.

"I'm not trying to make noise on purpose," I whisper back.

"Let me lead."

I shake my hands in exasperation. There's no way he could even get around me. The path is super narrow. I keep moving forward, inching my way slowly so as not to make any more noise. The path slopes up steeply, making my muscles ache. Like I said, I'm not much for physical activity. The air grows slightly cooler as we continue upward. I can no longer hear the kitchen.

Fortunately, the path opens into a slightly larger space. Unfortunately, it's a dead end.

CHAPTER 26

"WELL, THAT'S JUST GREAT," Zane says under his breath. "Nice going, Mizuno."

"Hey!" And then I lower my voice. "No one asked you to follow me, Yoshikawa."

"Whatever."

I turn my attention to the room. Maybe there's a way out. I hope there's a way out, because going back through the kitchen is a last resort, for sure.

It's dim in here, and I can barely see anything. I run my hands along the wall, trying to feel for a crevice or air flow. I need to get out of this cramped space before Zane annoys me even more.

But the wall is solid. I sit down and pull my knees against my chest, and Zane does the same. There's just barely enough room for the two of us, and we end up with our shoulders touching. I try to scoot away but can't. I sigh quietly.

How are we going to get out of here in time for next roll call at gym after lunch? I'm mad at myself for getting trapped here.

I'm also mad that Zane is with me. And that he seems so calm. His breathing, barely detectable, is even and he's completely still. I, on the other hand, keep shifting around.

"Stop moving so much," Zane says softly.

"You do you, I'll do me," I snap, keeping my voice low.

"Normally I wouldn't care what you do, but you're going to get us caught."

"How? Nobody knows we're here, and no one can hear us."

"You don't know that," Zane says in that know-it-all voice of his. "Every scrape of your foot, every knock of your elbow against the wall can reverberate."

I try to keep still, but the longer I sit here, the more anxious I feel.

"Are you claustrophobic?" Zane asks. "You're not about to have a panic attack, are you?"

"Like you care."

I feel him shrug. The seconds tick by. I prefer his annoying conversation to the silence, especially in the near darkness.

"I'm not claustrophobic," I say, finally. "But I hate being stuck in here."

"Same."

"But you're so calm." Still. Quiet.

I feel him shrug again. More seconds pass. I don't know why, but I'd rather be bickering.

"I know why you're here," I say.

"Yeah, genius, I followed you."

"No, I mean here, at Last Chance Academy."

Zane makes a sound.

"Did you just laugh?" I say incredulously. That was not the reaction I expected.

"It's not a secret," he says. "I'm pretty sure everyone knows. Besides, you gave that away when you told me to be ready to pick a lock last week."

"I thought that everyone's reason for being here is a secret."

"That kind of thing is hard to keep quiet," Zane says. "Being a criminal and all."

I scoff. "None of us are here because we're stellar, upstanding citizens."

"Yeah? What did you do, Mizuno? Is there a dead body somewhere?"

My breath catches. In my mind's eye I see Mom laid out in the coffin, looking like she's sleeping. Dad called her Sleeping Beauty, but no kiss from him, from me, from a fairy-tale prince would ever wake her up. I don't realize I'm crying until Zane snaps me out of my thoughts. For once he looks worried.

"Hey, hey, sorry. I shouldn't joke. That's why I don't talk to people. I always say the wrong thing."

I curse in Japanese as I quickly swipe my arm across my face.

Zane repeats the curse. "I know that word." And in a perfect imitation of Colette, he says, "A demerit for you, Ms. Mizuno."

I smile. Zane seems relieved, and he leans his head back against the wall.

"I'm not sorry I got caught," he says. "When I was a kid, sneaking through windows and taking things for my guardian felt like a game. The older I got, the better I got, but also I knew it was only a matter of time before I got busted. Being here is better than being in jail." Zane shrugs so big that I know he's doing it on purpose, to bug me.

"My mom died suddenly," I say. "I'm here because my grades suffered."

"So, like everyone else, you're not a criminal," he says.

"Really? How do you know why other students are here?" I ask. "I mean, this is Last Chance Academy. Every student is here because they were kicked out of at least one school. Maybe more."

"So, Mizuno, are you hunting for the next clue?" Zane

asks, changing the subject. "You still think this is just a fun treasure hunt with a free prize?"

"Why not?" I ask. "If you're so suspicious, then don't play."

"You'd like that, Mizuno. Narrow down the field. No chance."

We sit in silence for a few beats.

"What's the item you're supposed to find?" Zane asks.

"Something to do with my mom," I say. Then I want to kick myself. Zane caught me off guard, and I answered too quickly. This is what happens when it feels like a conversation between friends. We are not friends.

"Mine is home."

"This Mastermind knows things."

"Or it could just be luck that whatever they chose means something to us. If your clue had said 'home,' would it have struck you?"

I ponder that. It's possible. Tana's clue of "aunt" would have meant something to me too.

"What about the clue of language, though?" I ask. "Maybe it means 'words,' and maybe words mean books. Again. So maybe our things are hidden in a book but this time in our library? No. That wouldn't make sense. Would it?"

Zane doesn't answer. I glance at him. He's got his eyes closed. I doubt he's taking a nap. He's being smarter about this than I am. I'm thinking out loud, sharing theories with him, and he's back to being silent. Maybe he's figuring things out because I'm babbling and he's not sharing his thoughts with me. I clamp my mouth shut and tap my foot nervously.

That's when I feel the floor move.

CHAPTER 27

I LEAN FORWARD AND pry up a floorboard. Zane helps me. There's another toggle switch! I flip it, and the floor on Zane's side starts to move! I squeak as Zane crams himself next to me. When the floor opens, there's a dim light that reveals another slightly bigger room just below us.

It's a short drop. Zane takes the lead and slips down to the next level. I try to be as quiet as him, but I stumble and my feet scrape against the floor. A bright light streams in through a round window. I peer out and see the gardens on the side of the property. The walls are made of wood panels that I recognize from the state rooms. I go back to the opening we dropped through and look up. There's another switch on this side. I hit it so the floor closes.

When I return to where Zane is standing, I press my

ear to a panel and hear nothing. I make a silent wish, then press on the wall. It swings open, and Zane and I step into a state room. It's thankfully empty of any people, though it's full of tables and chairs. It looks like this state room is being used for storage. I shut the wall behind me. When I turn back around, I expect Zane to have disappeared, but he's standing there, looking at me. He tosses his head, and his long bangs flip off his forehead, out of his dark eyes.

"What?" I ask.

"You don't seem surprised."

"About?" I know he's talking about this secret room, but I don't want to give away that this is not the first secret room I've found.

"Fine." Zane walks to the doorway.

"Wait." I honestly don't expect him to, but he turns back to me. I don't even know why I told him to wait in the first place. "Um, good luck."

Zane nods, and then he steps out of the room, silent as always.

I glance at my watch. We lost over an hour and a half. Before I can keep looking, I have to get my backpack.

Fortunately, lost and found is staffed by rotating students and not the RAs. I thank Skye Cameron, a quiet sixth year, when she hands me my bag.

My backpack firmly on my back, I make my way to Jung Song's state room to put in my order for Sir Grey's things. I run into Winsome on my way in. We nod to each other as I step into the room. Is Winsome one of the ten still playing? I'm curious what she's getting from Jung. Wait. Maybe Jung is the person giving out the items? Is she running this game?

Jung has piles of books on Korean mythology. All ninth years have a big project due at the end of the year. But maybe these books are part of the clue. Do I have to say something in Korean? I don't know any Korean words! And that seems like an unfair clue. So maybe it's more general.

"Are you just going to stand there breathing loudly, or are you here to buy something?" Jung says.

"Korean is a language," I say unintentionally, still processing the clue out loud.

Jung narrows her eyes at me. "Are you being racist?"

"What? No!" I feel my face flame. Okay, so maybe Jung isn't part of the game. I quickly place my order and hand her cash.

I'm surprised when she pushes it back at me and says, "Barter."

I've been warned. "I'd rather pay cash."

Jung cocks her head and waits until I see that I don't have a choice.

"Fine. What do you want?" I ask.

"I want to know the details of the treasure hunt. Who finds the next items and what the clues are," she says.

"Why? You're not playing." Bold words, but her attitude makes me push back.

"I was right about you," she says.

"What do you mean?"

"You pay attention." Jung drums her fingers on the table. "You're right. I'm not playing. I have enough to keep me busy, and I don't care about winning the prize, but information is queen."

I realize that she holds all the cards, and now I know why she set up this little business. She probably doesn't need the cash. But she's made us reliant on her services and she knows things about us. She and Tana are the only ones who know I have a secret cat. A cat that could get me into big trouble.

"Okay, fine. But I need to know who the players are," I say. Like she says, information is queen, and Jung is the queen of information.

Jung smiles again, but this time it's full of respect. "You, Tana Rabin, Zane Yoshikawa, and Ryan Hsieh. But you know that already. Also, Paisley Schoenholz and Alice Watson, but Winsome Williams is helping her."

Right. Alice, who's a tenth year, and Winsome are cousins. That's six.

Jung continues, "Liam Parkison is the only eleventh year still playing, and then there's Kirby Anderson, Owen Reyes, and Wyatt McGuire, but his girlfriend, Kylie Faughnan, is helping him."

I tick off all the names, and teams, in my head. "It's a deal," I say, needing Sir Grey's supplies.

"You'll get your delivery by tomorrow night," Jung says.

Now not only am I trying to find my own dang item but I also have to somehow keep up with everyone else's movements. Actually, I would have done that anyway. It's good to know what the others are up to, and now I know who all the players are.

I'm not thrilled to have to share info with Jung, but she's right about one thing: I do pay attention. If anyone can track this treasure hunt, it's me.

CHAPTER 28

BY SUNDAY NOON I know where each of the players'
rooms are, and who their helpers are. Now all I have to do
is keep an eye on their windows to see if any items show
up next to the silver sun stickers. But I also need to look for
mine, or five players will definitely beat me out.

Midterms are coming up, and the assignments are getting more intense. If I'm to stay enrolled, I have to keep
my grades to a B average or higher. And avoid getting any
of those demerits that Colette keeps threatening. I need to
figure out where my item is today.

I start my search outdoors since I was checking windows
anyway. So far nobody has found anything. I kind of wish
someone had, because then maybe I'd have an idea of what I'm
looking for. When I see Winsome and Alice making their way

through the rose garden and then Kylie and Wyatt heading to the reflecting pool, I go back inside. Too crowded out here.

I wonder if the items are back on the administration side of the manor. That would stink. It was hard enough getting there the first time. I have no idea how everyone else managed to get the envelopes from the staff library, except for Ryan. I'll bet Ryan somehow charmed his way into that room.

"Anything?" Tana asks as we pass in opposite directions on the main staircase.

"Nada. You?"

"Nope."

I end up in the Grand Hall, empty this time. I lift the lid of the grand piano. Nothing in there. I stand on tiptoe to see if maybe something is tucked behind those grimacing statues. And that's when I remember the balcony. I back up to the opposite side of the long room. I can't see a doorway up there, but the balcony is as wide as my dorm room. Why have a large space but no way to get up there?

I cut through a room that's set up for some kind of banquet. The back door leads to a stairwell I recognize from my early days of exploration. The stairs lead down and away from the balcony, so I head the opposite way. I run into a few other students, but none of them is a player, so I ignore them.

Language is key. Language. Maybe I'm trying too hard. Mom's clues were tricky but not impossible. Language. I haven't checked any of the classrooms. Language arts!

I hurry to Ms. Yoo's room and methodically check every desk, every shelf, every book—and find nothing. I frown. I was so sure I was right.

Oh! There are two language arts rooms. Ms. Yoo teaches the lower school, from sixth year to eighth. I dash out of the room and to the upper-school classrooms, and search until I find a room that looks like it's for language arts. There are Shakespeare posters on the wall, and on the whiteboard is an essay topic.

I start at the back of the room, checking nooks and crannies, opening cabinets, and even peering into the trash can. When I hear voices, I dive under the teacher's desk and then feel silly. There's no rule that we can't be in the classrooms, and in fact, a couple of times Tana and I have camped out in Ms. Sheth's room to study.

Once the voices pass, I'm starting to back out when my hair snags on something. It's a silver envelope taped under the desk!

Leaving it stuck to the desk, I open the flap and find five tiny keys. My heart soars. I'm the first! I take a key. It's silver. Too small to fit into a door. I back out from under the desk and tuck the key into my sock before I leave the classroom.

I take a detour outside to do another check of the windows, and that's when I see something new by a sticker.

Someone has found their item.

CHAPTER 29

BUT HOW IS THAT possible? Unless that person returned the key after using it? Or maybe it's not the special item at all?

I take a breath to calm myself because it's hard to think straight when I'm spinning out. I look up at the window again. It's got two stickers. It's Ryan and Zane's room! I wish I could see the item better, but it's a small object and it's clearly next to the sticker. I hurry around to check all the windows. No other windows have anything next to a sticker.

Okay. It doesn't matter. There are still four more chances. *Think, Megumi, think!* The key is tiny. Too small for a door. And then it hits me. It's the perfect size for a padlock. There is a trunk with a padlock on it in the first secret room I discovered.

I try not to run because I don't want to alert anyone who might be watching. I quickly return to the fourth floor and skip over the creaky last step and walk down the darkened hall to the room overlooking the front of the school. Yes! No one is in here.

I open the wood panel easily this time and slip into the secret room. I pull the door mostly shut. I don't want to get trapped. At the back of the room is the locked trunk. Taking the key out of my sock, I squat in front of the padlock. This is it. I take a deep, steadying breath, a thrill shooting through me.

I slip the key into the lock, but it doesn't go all the way in. I jiggle and twist it, but nothing happens. My heart drops. This key doesn't fit this lock. I want to scream.

I take a beat. And then I examine the key again. There are tiny letters engraved on it, but I can't make out what it says.

Suddenly I hear footsteps behind me, and I leap up to face a very angry Jung Song.

"What are you doing in my room?" Her voice is a full-on growl.

"*Your* room?" I ask, recovering quickly. If this is her room, it's for sure not official.

She stalks forward, and I duck out of her path before she can plow into me. She peers at the lock, and confident that it remains locked, she whirls on me.

"What. Are. You. Doing. In. Here?" She bites out each word like it takes all her effort for her to not shout at me.

I can't afford to be on Jung's bad side. "Looking for the next thing for the treasure hunt."

"What makes you think it's in here?" Jung leans against the trunk. Her trunk, as is now obvious, and I'll bet that this is her secret stash, how she keeps students supplied. At least she looks less threatening now.

I hold up the tiny key.

"You're good," she says.

I flush with pleasure at the unexpected compliment. Then I remember our deal. "Either Ryan or Zane has found the actual item. I saw something displayed in their dorm window." It occurs to me just then that it has to be Zane. All five keys were in the envelope, but a key is needed to get the item. Zane can break in.

Jung's satisfied smile tells me that she's come to the same conclusion.

"I don't suppose you have a magnifying glass?" I ask, thinking of the tiny letters on the key.

When Jung goes back to the secret door, I think she's going to leave without answering me, but she shuts it instead.

"Face the door and no peeking," she commands.

I do as she says. I hear her open the chest and rummage around. The seconds that pass feel like minutes that feel like hours.

Finally Jung says, "Okay."

When I turn around, she shoves a gym bag at me. "What?" I ask.

"It's how I make my deliveries. If any staff member sees me, I'm just heading to or from the gym. Just drop off the bag to me in my state room."

I'm pretty sure anyone would see through me carrying a gym bag, but I nod. Jung pushes past me and peeks through a tiny crack. Satisfied, she pushes the door back open.

As I walk out, she growls, "Don't ever come in here again."

CHAPTER 30

ONCE I GET TO my room without running into anyone (Colette), Sir Grey comes out to greet me as always. I sit on the floor, give him a quick pat on the head, and then unzip the gym bag. On top is a towel and an empty water bottle. Underneath is my order for Sir Grey and a small magnifying glass. I put the kitty supplies away and sit at my desk. I turn on my lamp and peer at the key through the magnifying glass. I was wrong. Those aren't letters inscribed on the key but numbers.

751

A room number!

Tomorrow is Monday and I won't have time to hunt. I

rush out into the manor, giddy with anticipation. I'm going to get that item!

An hour later I'm breathing hard after looking everywhere I can think of, but I can't find a room 751. Could it be on the staff side of the manor? That seems totally unfair. Not that I expect any of this to be fair. I huff out a breath and make my way back to my room to think this over.

When I pass the library, I pause. The first clue was "Small print: good luck" and led to the staff library. This clue is "language is key." I found the key in the language arts classroom, but if I'm learning anything, it's that the Mastermind is tricky.

Language. Words. Library. When Zane and I were trapped together and I was thinking out loud, I'd guessed as much. Could I have been right?

I step into the empty room. I glance at the nearest shelf, and the numbers leap out at me: 751 isn't a room number. It's a call number!

I scurry through the library, skimming book spines until I get to the seven hundreds. I slow down, taking my time to read the numbers. Then I see it: 751. Art books on paintings. But which book? I start pulling out all the books with a call number starting with 751. My heart jumps. There's a small treasure chest on the shelf behind the books.

After stacking the books on the floor, I pull the chest to the edge of the shelf. It has a tiny lock. The key slips in easily and turns. I raise the lid, grinning so hard that my cheeks hurt.

Inside are random items. One of these things is mine and is supposed to represent my mom. How does the Mastermind even know what that would be? Will I know?

I need to work quickly before I get caught.

A pencil.

A blue feather.

A tiny ball of yarn.

An English Breakfast tea bag.

A toy convertible car.

A golf ball.

A packet of tomato seeds for planting.

A plastic dinosaur.

I gasp. It's not exactly the same as the yellow apatosaurus that's tucked into my duffel bag, the dinosaur I found on my treasure hunt with Mom, but it's a dinosaur. A green stegosaurus. I know it's mine. I slip it into my cardigan pocket. Just as I'm about to close the lid, I count the items. There are only eight, including my dinosaur. That means someone else in addition to Zane got here before me.

Who?

CHAPTER 31

I DON'T HAVE TO wait long to find out. When I get back to my room, Tana is there, and she looks too satisfied. I go quickly to our window, and sure enough there's something next to her silver sun sticker. A computer key, the letter X.

"I thought I beat you," I say, placing the dinosaur next to my sun sticker.

She grins big. "You shouldn't have left the magnifying glass on your desk."

Gah! I need to be more careful. That means Tana figured out that the numbers were a call number before I did. While I was wasting time checking room numbers, she was in the library. There can only be one winner, and it's clear that Tana is my biggest competitor.

With our items found and placed, Tana gets back to

her main priority, studying. She sits at her desk so swiftly that the first-place ribbons hanging from the shelf over her desk flutter. I walk over to look at them.

"You've won the spelling bee every year since you were in the first grade?" I ask.

Tana glances up from her math worksheet. "Well, not last year, since LCA doesn't have a spelling bee."

I point to a trophy. "First place in last year's science fair."

She tilts her face to me with a smile. "And I'll claim this year's too."

I shrug and walk to my desk. I don't care about that. I care about winning this treasure hunt.

Tana swivels her chair to me. "Have you done that extra-credit assignment about Leland Chase's family yet?"

I raise my eyebrows at her. "The assignment is for me. You can't get any credit for it." I'd forgotten about it, but I don't want Tana to get the jump on me on that, either.

"Fine," Tana says with a smile. "Feel like going over the last two chapters of social studies? I'll bet Ms. Maynor will give us a pop quiz on Tuesday."

I'm surprised. Not about a quiz but that Tana wants to study together. It's fine with me. Studying together doesn't mean we're BFFs. It's helping her as much as it's helping me, and like I said, I need to stay enrolled.

∗ ∗ ∗

On Monday when Tana and I walk into Life Skills, Ms. Sheth is waiting, and both Ryan and Zane are standing, not sitting.

"What's up?" Tana asks.

"We have an assembly, and we can't be late," Ms. Sheth says. "Let's go to the Angel Room."

The Angel Room overlooks the back gardens of the manor. Several rows of chairs with red cushions face a podium. Year seven is in the second row on the left. I sit between Ryan and Zane, with Tana on the aisle.

I glance around the room. Everyone else is business as usual. I don't sense any mad treasure hunt vibes. For whatever reason, the treasure hunt is nothing more than a fun game. But for the seventh years it seems to be more than that. For me because of Mom, and I want time to reconnect with Dad. For Tana because she needs to be the best. I wonder why Ryan and Zane are still playing with such intensity.

Dr. Ward steps up to the podium, and the noise level drops.

"Leland Chase Academy," she says. "We are honored this morning to have a special guest, an alumnus of our fine school and a great example of how education and experiences here can lead to success. I'm pleased to welcome the founder and CEO of Plum Blossom Express, Inc., William Hsieh."

A low murmur of excitement ripples through the room.

I may not be up on the latest companies, but everyone knows PBE, the high-end Asian food specialty company. It rocketed to success in under a year, and a lot of their items—like their sesame-bean balls and miso-almond cookies—sell out the minute they hit the shelves.

Wait. Did Dr. Ward say "Hsieh"? I glance at Ryan, and gone is that easygoing smile and the loose slump of his shoulders. He's sitting stiffly and wears a frown.

"Relative?" I ask.

"Brother," he answers, then crosses his arms across his chest.

Hmm. They aren't close, from what I can observe, plus it seems like Ryan had no idea his brother would be here.

We applaud as a man in an expensive suit steps up to the podium. While Ryan is pretty, his brother is handsome, with a strong jaw and sharp eyes. They have the same athletic build.

"Good morning, Leland Chase," he says in a pleasant enough voice, but not the warm, liquid voice Ryan has. "I started here in year ten as a rather troubled student, as I'm sure you are not surprised to hear. I graduated and attended Harvard and went on to receive my MBA from Wharton."

I feel more than hear Ryan sigh. With annoyance?

William goes on to list all his accolades, including awards and internships at companies we've all heard of.

He's surprisingly boring, and my mind wanders to the most pressing issue. Who will remain in the treasure hunt? Ryan has to know that Zane has found his item. The question is, will Zane tell Ryan where to find his? I doubt it. I mean, Tana and I are much friendlier with each other, and neither of us would share information on purpose. Plus, Zane didn't need the key, but Ryan would.

Who will the rest of the five be? And what will the next envelope reveal? The treasure hunt has to end before winter break, since the prize is to travel over school vacation. How many more rounds will there be? And what's the point of this? This Mastermind is putting in a lot of work to run this treasure hunt to give away a big prize. Is there a catch? If it were being run by the school, I could see it being like a weekend activity, something to give us a break from studies. But it can't be run by the school, since we're not allowed to be caught.

I'm jolted out of my thoughts when the room breaks into applause. William smiles and nods to the room, but his eyes don't catch Ryan's.

Dr. Ward joins William at the podium and thanks him. She fastens her piercing gaze on us and says, "This is proof that each one of you can be a success. There is no reason you can't excel at whatever you choose. Do not squander this very valuable opportunity."

It's interesting how she can make that sound more like

a threat than encouragement. She excuses us to return to our classes, but a few students, mostly twelfth years, approach William.

"Aren't you going to talk to him?" I ask Ryan.

"Nope."

We shuffle to the rear of the room to join Ms. Sheth, and head down the hall to return to our classroom. Ryan and I fall back as some eighth years cut us off in their hurry to get to their classroom.

"What? No hug for your big brother?" A voice comes from behind us and freezes Ryan in place.

I stop too. Ryan heaves a sigh and turns to face his brother. "Hey, Will."

"Dr. Ward says you're doing well in classes," William says as if he's more a parent than a sibling. There seems to be a big age difference. Ryan's brother turns to me with raised eyebrows.

"This is Meg Mizuno," Ryan says.

William nods once at me and turns back to Ryan. "Stay out of trouble and stop trying to skate by. Don't bring shame onto the Hsieh name."

And with that, William leaves.

A million questions pop into my head as Ryan and I walk to class, but I don't say a word. For the first time there is nothing inviting or warm about Ryan Hsieh.

CHAPTER 32

I DON'T GET ANOTHER chance to ask Ryan about his brother. Midterms are coming up fast, and I need to focus on studying and writing an essay for Ms. Yoo's class.

Monday afternoon I am finally officially starting my independent study. I meet Carole by the fountain that marks the entrance to the main flower garden. There aren't any flowers blooming now, of course, and the garden is brown and barren.

Carole sits on a wood bench to the right of the fountain, which is a big stone cherub holding a tilted pitcher. In the warmer months water flows from the pitcher into the pool below.

When Carole sees me, she smiles and waves. "Meg, it's nice to finally get to spend time with you." She pats the seat next to her. She has dark brown hair in a pixie cut that reveals a line of silver studs around her ears. It's cold out, but she wears no hat or scarf, while I'm bundled up in my long down coat, an LCA scarf, and a knit hat jammed onto my head.

I sit next to her and tighten the scarf around my neck.

"Are you going to be okay outside?" she asks.

"I'm not a big fan of the outdoors," I admit. "I chose this as my IS because I want to learn more."

I'm surprised when Carole says, "That's fabulous!"

"It is?"

"Yes. You're coming with a beginner's mind, open and ready to learn. That's better than my having to undo years of untruths or dealing with entitled arrogance."

"Um."

She laughs. "Sorry! I've been told I'm very opinionated and blunt."

"I can handle that," I say.

"Then we're going to get along fine."

We spend the next hour just talking and walking through the gardens. I think Carole suggested walking because I was starting to shiver while we were sitting. We don't talk about nature or wildlife. Instead she tells me about her background.

Her mother's side is Ojibwe, and her father is mostly English. Carole's love of the outdoors comes from her mother. It turns out Carole is new to LCA, hired at the same time as Ms. Sheth in LCA's effort to be more diverse, apparently. She is here at LCA only a few hours a week, but now that she's my IS sponsor, she'll be at LCA more often. Her main job is as a curator at an art museum, trying to build a collection of local Native art. Art that's properly procured and wasn't stolen, as she explains to me. In just an hour I learn more about colonialism and the misinformation I've been fed in school about Indigenous people than I learned in my years of public-school education.

At the end of our session, Carole reaches into her bag and pulls out a pair of binoculars.

"These aren't fancy," she says as she hands them to me, "but they will do the job. Tomorrow we'll start looking for wildlife and birds. Even in winter there is plenty to see. I'll teach you how to identify tracks and other signs that wildlife leave. Like clues."

Clues! I smile as I loop the strap of the binoculars around my neck. I just thought of the perfect use for these.

CHAPTER 33

WHEN I DROP THE gym bag off to Jung, she asks for an update. Thanks to the binoculars, I have one.

"Plastic dinosaur for me, computer key for Tana, padlock for Zane, pencil for Ryan, and a golf ball for Wyatt," I say. I'm curious what the pencil means for Ryan. The golf ball is obvious, as it's no secret that Wyatt is obsessed with golf.

"We're even now," I say.

Jung raises her eyebrows. "Are we?"

"Until I need to buy something else." I bartered info for Sir Grey's supplies, but I'm good for at least a month. And now I hold some cards too. Jung wants information, and I can supply it to her. Although, I'm probably not the first student who is trying to game her system.

✳ ✳ ✳

The rest of the week flies by as the entire student body sinks into preparing for midterms. It's all studying, all the time. I won't lie. It's INTENSE. I have never studied so hard with hardly any breaks. It helps having Tana as my roommate. She basically studies nonstop anyway.

But by Saturday night, even Tana agrees that we need a break. Activity nights and IS are suspended, but at dinner we tell the guys to meet us in the Green Room, where activity nights normally take place.

Ryan and Zane are already there when Tana and I arrive. They have dumped a box of puzzle pieces onto the large table and are putting together the edges. I see from the box top that it's a tropical jungle setting with brightly colored flowers and birds.

"Hmm," I say. "I didn't peg either of you as puzzle people."

Ryan quirks an eyebrow. "What do puzzle people look like?"

"Not you," I snap back with a laugh.

"You're in a good mood, Mizuno," Zane deadpans without looking up at me. He's intensely searching for an edge piece.

I glance at Tana, who is already putting together a section of the puzzle. Not the edge. Rebel.

"Oh, it's because I'll probably outscore Tana on the social studies test," I say.

Ryan, Zane, and I all laugh at the same time when Tana whips her head up at me, a challenge in her eyes. She relaxes and says, "Very funny."

"Because nobody beats Tana Rabin," Ryan says in an announcer voice.

Tana sighs. "I don't know. Meg has been studying a lot, and in our last study session she matched me point for point."

"That still bothering you?" I ask. That was on Monday night.

"I might have to get your extra-credit points from Ms. Sheth after all to raise my score," Tana says, grinning.

I wrinkle my nose at her. She may be teasing, but I'm starting to worry she might really go for it. I didn't want the extra work, but I don't want Tana to scoop me either. Maybe I should research Leland Chase's family after midterms.

"Anyone want to wager who takes the top score next week?" Ryan asks.

"I'm not taking that bet," Zane says.

Ryan glances at me and Tana, and we both shake our heads.

It takes us an hour, but we finish putting the puzzle together. We talk about music—pop for Tana, indie rock for Ryan, J-pop for me, and Zane doesn't answer; movies— we all agree we love action thrillers, and I keep it to myself that Mom and I used to watch period romances; and spectator sports—soccer for Zane, basketball for Ryan, and nothing of note for me or Tana. It's nice to not talk about midterms for an hour. Come Monday we'll be in full-fledged test mode.

When Tana and I get back to our room, Sir Grey greets us as always. Tana, unsurprisingly, pulls out her notes for math and starts going over the problem sets. I'm feeling burnt out and restless. Doing the puzzle stilled my mind and calmed me. I'm not an anxious test-taker, but the seriousness of everyone studying makes me antsy.

I glance at Tana. She's got her back to me and is hunched over her desk, scribbling on paper. I know what I need to do to calm myself. It's something I haven't done in a while. I reach under my bed and quietly drag out my duffel bag. I unzip it and retrieve a few sheets of origami paper. After I slide my bag back under my bed, I move to my desk and lose myself in folding.

"Oh! That's so cute! Is that a bird?"

Tana's voice startles me. I flinch as her hand reaches over my shoulder for the first item I folded.

She sits on my bed and turns the yellow origami bird over. "How did you do this? This is amazing!"

I make a last fold on the blue paper to make a cat. "It's origami," I say. "My mom taught me when I was little, and I became obsessed."

"Will you teach me?" Tana asks, her eyes bright.

"No." The word snaps out of me before I have a chance to stop it.

Tana makes a sound. I've hurt her feelings. I shouldn't care. I don't want to care, but I do. "Sorry," I say. "Kind of a knee-jerk reaction."

"Because of your mom? I get it. Sorry. It must be hard." Tana places the bird back on my desk.

I know that the kind thing would be to give it to her, but I am afraid. I'm afraid of what that symbolizes and what it reminds me of. But Tana and I have been spending most of our time together, especially this past week. Being at LCA could have been miserable, but it's not. Because of her.

"It's not because of my mom," I say softly. I take a fresh piece of paper and start to fold.

"No?"

I concentrate on making precise folds as I talk. "I used to make origami for Addy. She was my best friend. She said she loved the origami I made for her."

Tana is silent, but I know she's listening.

"After my mom died, Addy got impatient with me and said I was no fun to be around anymore."

At that, Tana does make a sound, like she's shocked and angry.

I push myself to finish. "We stopped being friends. I moved to my aunt's for all of sixth grade. I texted Addy a few times, but she never responded. During spring break I went to her house. I wanted to make up with her. We'd been inseparable for most of our lives. When she answered the door, I handed her all the origami I'd been making for her since I'd left for my aunt's. There were maybe fifty? Anyway, she laughed and said she didn't want my cheap paper crafts and that she'd only been pretending to like them."

I mean to go on, but I can't. I want to say out loud how much that hurt. But I can't say the words that are lodged in my throat.

"Oh, Meg," Tana says. "What a complete witch! She doesn't deserve your friendship!"

Her voice is so full of anger and venom that I'm both shocked and pleased. I look down at my finished origami. A tulip. One of the first things I taught myself.

I turn and put the flower into Tana's lap. She picks it up with such reverence that I almost laugh. Almost.

Her eyes shine. "I would never, ever treat you like that, Meg," she says. "I promise, I am your friend, and you can trust me. Always."

She returns to her desk and puts the origami tulip on the shelf above her desk. The only thing that's not a first-place ribbon or trophy.

We spend the rest of the evening in silence, studying. When we climb into bed at lights-out, Tana, as always, says, "Good night, Meg."

And for the first time I respond. "Good night, Tana."

CHAPTER 34

MIDTERMS LAST A FULL week. By the time I hit send on one of the school computers for my essay to Ms. Yoo on Friday, I'm completely exhausted.

Activity night is back on, and it's a dull foreign film. Most of us fall asleep, but maybe it's because we're all so tired. Not the best reward for midterm week, but there's a Halloween party tomorrow.

Tana and I head back to our room. We haven't talked about origami or Addy since Saturday, but last I saw this morning, the tulip I made for her remains on her shelf.

"How do you think you did on midterms?" Tana asks.

"Excellent!" I say to tease her. Actually, I think I did pretty well, and I look forward to sharing my grades with Dad. Hearing some pride in his voice will definitely be better than the disappointment in his eyes when I was failing in sixth grade.

Tana sniffs but doesn't say anything else about that. "At least the film let us catch up a little on sleep," she says.

"At least." I'm going to need to sleep for another day to catch up. Sleeping in is the perfect reward.

"We need to talk about our costumes."

"Our what?" I shoot her a look.

"The Halloween party!" She's bouncing along as we walk, as if the two-hour nap during the movie made up for her lack of sleep over the past two weeks. "We're too late to order anything, so we'll have to cobble something together from our closets."

"Tana," I say, trying not to sound exasperated. "If you wanted to dress up, why didn't you plan ahead?"

"We were studying!" She drops her voice to a whisper. "And focused on other things."

I don't do costumes, and I don't do parties. But it's not like I can avoid it. The party is the sanctioned Saturday night activity. Roll is taken. Participation counts. "Fine."

"Yay!" Tana claps her hands as we get to our room.

When Tana opens our door, on the floor is a silver envelope. We step in quickly and lock our door. We have an hour before room check. Tana scoops up the envelope.

"That's weird," she says, showing me her name on the envelope. "Where's yours?"

We search under our beds, in case it slid across the room. We check our closets in case Sir Grey took it. But there is no second envelope.

"Maybe this is for both of us?" Tana suggests.

I seriously doubt it, but I wave at her. "Go ahead and open it. Maybe it will say something about mine."

We sit on the floor between our beds, and Tana opens the envelope. She pulls out the charcoal-colored card, and I watch her face as she reads it. Her eyes skim back and forth and then stop. She frowns.

"What?" I ask.

"It makes no sense!" Tana reads out loud, "Congratulations, Tana, on making it this far. Only four will remain after this, so be quick. This one has two parts. Signed, the Mastermind."

"That's it?" I ask.

She hands the card to me. When I see a jumble of letters on the bottom half of the card, I grin. A cipher! Finally the clues are getting more challenging.

Tana smacks me playfully on the shoulder. "You know what it means," she says. Then she takes her card back. "Don't worry. I'll figure it out!"

But I *am* worried. While I could try to figure out the cipher on her card, what if that clue is specifically for her and not a general clue for all the players? I need to find my envelope.

CHAPTER 35

WHEN I WAKE UP the next morning, I'm surprised Tana is still in bed. She's awake, though, and scribbling in her notebook. She smiles at me when she realizes I'm watching her.

"It's some sort of code, right?" Tana points her pen to the charcoal-colored clue card on her lap.

I shrug.

She grins. "Thought so! I'll figure it out." Then she puts her pen down and turns her full attention on me. "What are you going to do about your envelope? Maybe there was a mistake and it got delivered to the wrong door?"

"Yeah, I thought of that." I can knock on doors. I glance at the clock. Nine isn't too early, right?

I change into my uniform while Tana moves to her desk to continue puzzling out her clue. I need to move quickly. Only four of us will move on to the next step.

"I'll be back. With my envelope," I promise. A friendly threat.

"Wait," she says. "What about our costumes for tonight's party?"

I sigh. "Black cats? I have plenty of black clothes."

"Brilliant! And I have makeup for whiskers and pink noses. We'll be adorable." She smiles. "I'm sure Ryan and Zane will think so too."

Hmm. I don't really care about that. I wonder for a brief moment, though, what Ryan will look like in a costume. Like a dashing prince or something. I can't even begin to imagine Zane in a costume. It will be worth going to the party to see that!

The hall is silent as I make my way to the far end, away from Colette's room. I knock softly on Zarifa and Paisley's door. I hear quiet footfalls, and the door eases open. Zarifa looks surprised to see me. We've never talked, other than greetings when we pass one another or run into each other in the bathroom.

"Hey," I say in a low voice. "Sorry to bug you, but did you get something meant for me?"

Zarifa raises an eyebrow and shakes her head. "You mean an envelope?" she whispers.

"Yeah. Mine seems to have gone missing." I hate admitting that. It feels like a failure even though it's not my fault. At least I don't think it is.

"Meg Mizuno." A wholly too familiar and unwelcome voice bounces down the hall to me.

Zarifa's eyes widen. "I can't get any more demerits," she says, shutting her door.

There is no rule against talking in the halls during the day or knocking on doors, so I don't see how Colette can give any demerits out for this. But then again, it *is* Colette. She can find any reason to hand out demerits.

Colette stands with her hands on her hips at the other end of the hallway. I make my way over to her, wondering what rule I could have possibly broken. I've escaped getting any demerits up till now, but I know it's only a matter of time before she has her way.

"Come in," she commands.

I step into the room warily, expecting a dungeon. I'm surprised that the room is bright and airy, with dried flowers in tiny pottery vases on her desk and shelves. On her nightstand is a larger ceramic vase painted in swirls of oranges and blues. There are no photos. I mean, it's not like I have friends back home, but I have two pictures on my desk, one of me and Mom from the last Girl's Day we spent together; and one of me, Mom, and Dad from New Year's when I was eight and we went to Japan.

"Sit." Colette points to a desk chair on the other side of the room.

I take a deep breath to calm myself.

"I can't figure you out, Meg," Colette says with a frown. "You keep to yourself for the most part, you stay out of trouble, and you've avoided getting any demerits."

I know that's not unusual. Most of the student body is pretty focused on staying enrolled and out of trouble. LCA gets rid of troublemakers quickly, from what I've heard. I wonder why Colette wants to give us all so much grief.

"Maybe you're an RA in the making," Colette says, sitting down on her desk chair, facing me.

"What?"

"You're a rule follower."

Again, that's not a big departure from other students. Other than Jung. She out of everyone takes the biggest risks. At least that I know of. I haven't gotten to know many of the other students.

"Maybe you're on track to do bigger things," Colette says, giving me a creepy smile, like we're partners or something. (Not friends. She has none as far as I can tell.)

I'm losing time here. I need to look for my envelope. Time to hurry this along. "Sure," I say with a probably equally creepy smile.

"I thought so," Colette says with a satisfied nod. "You and I are alike."

What? No. Not at all, but I keep my smile on my face. Hurry up and spit it out, Colette!

"What is this all about?" I ask.

Colette reaches into the top drawer of her desk and pulls out a silver envelope. It has my name on it.

CHAPTER 36

"WHAT IS THIS?" COLETTE asks, flapping the envelope at me.

I shake off my shock and answer calmly, "It looks like an envelope addressed to me. So, I guess the real question is, why do *you* have it?"

She narrows her eyes at me. "Don't get smart with me, Meg. I've seen a couple of students with these same envelopes."

"Is there a rule against writing letters to each other?" I stand up and hold my hand out. I don't want to give her a chance to continue interrogating me. And at least now I know she hasn't opened it.

"Are you sure you don't want to tell me anything?" Colette holds the envelope just out of reach.

"There's nothing to tell. It's a private note to me."

"I'm disappointed, Meg. Here I thought we had an understanding. I could write you a glowing recommendation to be RA when you hit eleventh year."

"Why would I want that?" I ask before I can stop myself. It's a serious question. Why would I want the extra responsibility and to set myself apart from the others, and not in a good way? Although, Oliver seems to be well-liked enough.

Colette waves her free hand, the one not holding my envelope, toward her room. "A guaranteed single for both eleventh and twelfth years, for one. Access to the staff library and computer lab. Those computers are much nicer and newer."

Maybe Tana would want to be RA, then.

"And," Colette continues, "pretty much free run of the manor and a lot of other perks."

"Hmm." I have absolutely zero intention of being here in eleventh year anyway. If all goes according to plan, I'll be back home living with Dad by next year. But first I need to win this treasure hunt.

I hold out my hand.

Colette shakes her head. "Maybe you're not as smart as I thought you were."

No. I'm smarter.

She slaps the envelope into my open hand. "There's

something strange going on, and if I find out you're at the center of it, I will get you expelled so fast, it will make your head spin."

Expelled would mean homeschooling with evil Aunt Vivian. Winning will mean living with Dad.

"I'm not at the center of anything," I say truthfully, and I try to act casual about the envelope, holding it loosely in my hand, like it isn't the key to my happiness.

"I'm watching you," Colette says, and nods at her door, dismissing me.

CHAPTER 37

ONCE I'M SAFELY INSIDE my room, I lock the door and tear into my envelope. Tana is gone. Did she figure out the code?

Congratulations, Meg, on making it this far.
Only four will remain after this, so be quick.
This one has two parts.
~The Mastermind

Wms'pc yl cvncpr yr qrsbw.
Lmr ajcyp rm mrfcpq, zsr mztgmsq rm wms.
Wms ilmu ufyr rm bm ugrf rfc grck.
Fsppw.

It is a cipher, just like on Tana's note! I grab a notebook and pen. Mom started using ciphers when I turned eight. They were fun puzzles and were some of my favorite treasure hunt clues. Mom gave up using them a year later because she noted I was too good at solving them.

When Mom used a cipher, she included a clue to the key, always a number to tell me how many letters of the alphabet to move over. There are two numbers in the note, four and two. I try four first, and the cipher makes zero sense, so I try two, which is underlined. And that's it.

As I decode the message, I take my time, even though I want to rush. I'm worried that Tana has a big lead on me. But messing up and starting over will take even more time. Letter by letter, double-checking as I go, I write out the translation.

> You're an expert at study.
> Not clear to others but obvious to you.
> You know what to do with the item.
> Hurry.

Great. I'm already feeling behind, and part of the clue tells me to hurry. I take a deep breath and read it over again.

Expert at study. We were all studying madly. Is the Mastermind referring to midterms? But why wait till after the exams are over, then?

I move on to the next line. Not clear to others but obvious to me. Gah. I don't know what to make of that, either.

At least the third line makes sense immediately. Whatever I find goes into the window with the rest of my collection. But I need to find it first.

Tana returns to the room, and I close my notebook before turning to her. She looks frustrated. Good. That means she hasn't found her item yet.

She waves her card at me. "It makes no sense!"

Ah, she hasn't figured out the cipher! I'm ahead of her! I keep my face a neutral mask, and she raises her eyebrows at me.

"Did you find your envelope?" she asks.

I nod and give her the rundown about Colette.

Tana shakes her head. "She's so shady. How did she even get your envelope?"

"I'm guessing it was sticking out from under our door." If she had broken in, she would have taken Tana's, too. "This means she's paying attention," I continue. "We have to be more careful than ever. Besides the fact that the Mastermind will shut the game down if any administrators find out."

"Have you figured out the clue?"

"Maybe."

She laughs. "Okay, fair enough! I'd better get to it." Tana packs up her backpack, tucking her card into an inside pocket, and leaves the room. I bet she'll use the computer to figure out the code. Maybe make up a program to decipher it. She's an expert there, and you might as well use your expertise to your advantage.

Expert. Expert at study. Tana's individual study is computer programming. That's the answer to the first line of the clue!

I groan out loud, startling Sir Grey, who was purring on my pillow. He gives me a haughty look and struts to his spot in the closet, reminding me that I need to take out his trash. Outside. Because that's my independent study, and if I'm right about the clue, then that means my item will be someplace outside. I'm definitely not even close to being an expert, but I suppose the Mastermind doesn't care.

As I clean Sir Grey's litter box, I ponder who the Mastermind could be. Someone on campus because otherwise how would the envelopes get to us and how would this person know anything about us, including who gets the clues into the windows?

Maybe it's a twelfth year, since twelfth years are not included. But that doesn't really make sense. Could it be a teacher? I don't think the teachers have enough money to give away a trip as a prize. It has to be the school. A reward for the cleverest of us?

Okay, that's not the most important thing to figure out. I need to find my item somewhere outdoors. I groan again.

The outdoors is way too large. How am I ever going to find whatever it is?

But the clock is ticking. Tana may not know how to figure out the key for the cipher, but she's brilliant with computers, and she will create a program to decipher the code for sure.

Even though we are friends now . . . I can't let her beat me.

CHAPTER 38

AFTER DUMPING SIR GREY'S trash, I head over to the garden area. I'm going to assume that the Mastermind isn't going to make this impossible.

Not clear to others but obvious to you. Obvious to me? I haven't been meeting with Carole long and in fact haven't seen her in two weeks. I only met with her for a week before midterm studies got underway. Where do I even start?

The bench! I always met Carole at the bench.

I hurry to it and search, including underneath, but see nothing. Could I be wrong? Maybe I need to be sitting. I face the fountain. The water has been turned off for weeks. I get up and look around the fountain and inside it.

"What are you doing, Meg?" Ryan squats next to me where I'm squinting at the bottom of the fountain's pool.

I stand to give my knees a break and keep Ryan from possibly finding my clue. "Nothing," I say with a smile, knowing full well that he knows I'm not doing nothing.

"Did you figure out what the clue card says?" He stands too, facing me with that smile on his too-pretty face.

"Did you?" I counter.

He laughs. "Ah, Meg. You are predictable. Lovable but predictable."

My heart leaps when he says "lovable," even though I know he doesn't mean it literally. Besides, I think Tana might have a crush on him. NOT that I have a crush! *Focus, Megumi!*

"I can't even figure out what the card says." Ryan sighs. "I'm sure you have, though. Otherwise what are you doing out here?"

"Maybe I'm taking a walk," I say.

"You're hardly ever outside," he says. "Except when you're meeting with Carole. Something to do with your IS, right? Is that the clue?"

Ugh. Ryan is more observant than I gave him credit for. I struggle to keep my face impassive, but Ryan sees my annoyance.

He chortles. "I'm right!"

I roll my eyes. "What *is* your IS anyway? It's only fair,

since you seem to know mine and maybe your nosiness got you a hint."

"You want to take a guess?"

I recall that his item in the window is a pencil. "Something to do with writing."

Ryan's eyebrows shoot up in surprise.

"I'm right!" I say. "What kind of writing?"

"I'm sure you'll figure it out on your own," he says.

"Romances!" I say, laughing. "You're Jane Austen remade!"

This time he rolls his eyes.

I frown. "There's nothing wrong with Jane Austen!"

"I didn't say there was," Ryan says, raising his eyebrows. "I'll say this much. While I may not write about romances, I'm very good at romancing."

My face flushes, and he laughs.

"You're fun to tease, Meg."

I stick my tongue out at him, like I'm five.

"Aw, don't be mad," he says. "My IS isn't a secret, but I don't like to talk about it."

"Why not?"

He shrugs. "I'm still exploring."

"Have you shared your writing with anyone? Can I read something?" I'm suddenly very interested to know what Ryan Hsieh writes about.

"Maybe someday."

I smile. "Someday" is a nice promise.

"Well, I'm off to find something to do with my IS," Ryan says with a salute. "Thanks for the help!"

"Not intentional!" I say with a huff.

He flashes me one more smile, then hurries back toward the manor.

I circle the fountain two more times and give up. I follow the path into the garden. Carole hasn't taken me onto the nature trails yet. We started with the flowers and plants in the cultivated garden. What little there was to see. She told me that a good naturalist can identify plants without the flowers blooming. Well, I am not a good naturalist.

Carole also pointed out some birds to me. Oh! My binoculars! Maybe I need them to find my item! I check my watch just as my stomach rumbles. I skipped breakfast and forgot to order more energy bars from the online school shop. That means I need to swing by the buffet before grabbing my binoculars. I hate to lose time, but low blood sugar means I can't think clearly.

While I'm scarfing down a bowl of cereal, Zane sits across from me. That's not entirely surprising. What *is* surprising is his nudging me under the table with his foot. Twice. Because the first time I assumed it was an accident.

I look up from my bowl, chewing and then swallowing the last of my cereal.

"Twitchy foot, Yoshikawa?" I ask quietly.

He smirks. "Interesting cipher," he says, surprising me a second time.

What is wrong with these boys? Why can't they just stick to themselves and work on the treasure hunt without involving me?

"You *do* know this is a competition, right?" I ask, wiping my mouth with the cloth napkin.

"Four move on. It's going to be the seventh years," he says.

"How do you know?"

Zane peels an orange expertly. As usual, his plate is filled with food. It makes me wonder if he didn't have access to meals when he was living with that family "friend." It's hard not to feel bad for him, though I know he'd hate pity.

His easy demeanor right now means either he has already found his item or he doesn't feel any pressure to hurry.

"Yoshikawa," I say, impatient to get out of here and back to my own search. "Spill."

"Wyatt isn't playing anymore," Zane says. "Because Kylie doesn't want him to."

I narrow my eyes at him. If I ever got a boyfriend, and that's a big "if" since I don't want one, I wouldn't make them give up things that are important to them. But who knows? Maybe the game isn't that important to Wyatt. Like I said, most of the student body seems to have moved on without any hard feelings.

"Okay," I say, standing up to bus my bowl and glass. "But even so, we still need to find our items."

He smiles. "So, you haven't found yours yet."

Gah! I quickly dump my dirty dishes into the bin and flounce out of the dining room.

CHAPTER 39

FORTUNATELY, STUDY HALL IS canceled while volunteer students and staff set up for tonight's Halloween party, so I can look for my item after gym. In my room I quickly change out of my gym clothes and back into my uniform, making sure to tuck my binoculars into my backpack.

Just as I open the door to head out, Tana comes in. She is glowing.

I close the door behind her. "You found your item," I say.

She grins. "You?"

"Almost."

"Just to be clear, this makes two I found before you." She says this with a light voice. She's teasing, but also crowing.

"The only one that really counts is the last one," I say.

"So true."

I hurry outside. Even if what Zane said about Wyatt no longer playing is true, I still don't want to be last. I sit on the bench in front of the fountain and pull out my binoculars. I train them on the fountain. Nothing. Not clear to others but obvious to me. It's going to be something that isn't easily spotted. I start down the path through the garden. The last session with Carole was about identifying birds. When I reach the part of the garden that butts up against the woods, I see something fluttering in a tree. I look through the binoculars and smile.

"Male cardinal," I say softly to myself. It's my first official bird identification on my own. I dig into my backpack for the notebook Carole gave me to keep a birding list. I carefully write the date, location, and bird.

I raise the binoculars to my eyes again and scan for more birds, and that's when I spot something that doesn't belong. Tucked into the crook of a branch is a small silver-colored box. It's too high up for me to reach. I circle the tree, and on the opposite side of the path is a knob on the trunk that could be used as a step to climb the tree. Except I don't climb trees.

"You do now," I say to myself.

I put my backpack and binoculars down, step up onto the knobby projection of the trunk, and search for a handhold. I have to push off the ground with my other foot to leap high enough to try to grab the lowest branch. It takes four tries, but I finally grasp the branch with one hand while precariously balancing on the trunk. My other foot flails about until I'm able to wrap my other hand around the branch too. I'm now panting like I've run five miles. (Note: I can't even run one mile.) If I fall, I won't have the energy to try again.

I pull with all my strength and swing my leg over the branch. I almost shout with triumph, except I have no extra breath for that. I straddle the branch, careful not to look down. I don't think I'm afraid of heights, but now is not the time to find out. Also, the skirts of these uniforms make it hard to climb, but I'm glad for the LCA-approved leggings we can wear on colder days.

I scoot along the branch until I'm at the trunk and can reach the next branch above me, where the box is nestled. I stand and pat around blindly above me. My hand connects with the cardboard box, and I close my fingers around it. Now I have to figure out how to climb down with only one hand. But how?

The solution comes when I suddenly hear my name shouted. I'm so startled that I fall out of the tree and land on my butt, on soft ground, thankfully.

"Detention!" Colette shouts with glee.

I stand up and brush myself off with one hand, while keeping the hand with the box behind me. "I'm not injured. Thank you for your concern," I say.

"I'm afraid you won't be able to attend the Halloween party," she says with a big smile. "You'll stay in Dr. Ward's office after dinner."

That's hardly punishment at all. I don't care about a party, and now I'll have time to consider next steps for winning this treasure hunt. But I make sure to look unhappy about it.

CHAPTER 40

BACK IN MY ROOM I open my box. Inside is a silver bird. As I place it on the windowsill, I see Tana's item. A silver mouse. Is this an animal theme, or a clever play on a computer mouse?

When Tana returns to our room, she checks our windowsill and says, "Congratulations!"

"Don't get too confident," I say.

She laughs. "Too late!" Then she nods. "I'm glad you got your envelope."

"I have some bad news." I tell Tana about detention and having to miss the party.

"That's not fair! There are no rules against climbing trees," she says. "I don't think."

I shrug. "I didn't ask what rule I'd broken. I had the box

in my hand and didn't want to spend any extra time with her." I feel a little bad, since I know Tana was excited about having matching costumes.

"That stinks, Meg," Tana says with a sad face. "You're going to miss the party."

Oh. She's not upset about the costume thing. She's upset for me. That's nice. But unnecessary.

"It's fine. Maybe my dad will be extra chatty on our call." And either way, I can ponder my strategy to win this thing.

"I'm disappointed to hear you have detention for being in a restricted area," Dr. Ward says when I get to her office after dinner.

I'm unsure if being in a tree really is restricted or if Colette was being vague to Dr. Ward about the reason for giving me detention, but I don't really care enough to ask.

"But," Dr. Ward continues, "you will still get your call with your father, as it's a condition he arranged."

I didn't even think that my call might be taken away. I'm relieved and grateful. That feeling doesn't last long.

"I'm sorry, Megumi," Dad says. "I have to be in India over Thanksgiving week, but Aunt Vivian is happy to have you for the holiday. I can send a car to pick you up."

My heart falls. I was looking forward to seeing Dad. But there's no way I want to spend any time with Aunt

Vivian. I think quickly and realize that staying at school over Thanksgiving break might give me an advantage toward winning.

I take a deep breath and am proud when my voice doesn't waver. "No, it's okay, Dad. I'll stay here. But you're going to be home for Christmas, right?" That is the most important thing of all.

"Of course, Megumi. I'm looking forward to it."

"And you haven't put the house on the market yet?"

"No," Dad says in an overly gentle tone. "I told you we'd pack up together over the winter break."

He makes it sound like he's doing me a favor or that it will be some kind of special bonding activity. Little does he know, I intend for us to have a much better activity, and I'll convince him to keep our house and let me move home.

When we get off the call, I sigh. I wish Dad could read my mind and know what I'm thinking. I wish he knew how much I want to come home and how I need him to be my dad still. But it's too hard to talk to him. Mom was always the person I went to with everything. Maybe it's too much to expect Dad to be Mom.

Detention means I have to remain in this room during the Halloween party. I can hear Dr. Ward on the phone behind closed doors. I don't intend to eavesdrop, but her voice gets louder, and I can't help it.

"It's vital that we get more money!" she nearly shouts.

"Get the donors to come through! Find more donors! Do something!"

And then silence. Is the school in financial trouble? I noticed that some of the classrooms need a paint job. Maybe the school isn't behind the treasure hunt after all. If they're hurting for money, why would they give away a free vacation?

I'm focusing on the wrong thing. It doesn't matter who is running it. What really matters is that I win.

CHAPTER 41

THE WEEK DRAGS AS we wait for the next envelope. As Zane predicted, we four seventh years are the remaining players. Colette dogs my heels, but I make sure to be the perfect LCA student, following rules to the extreme.

Friday night's activity is another movie. Tana and I race for the big couch. It's the most comfortable, but more important, it fits the four of us. Someone passes us and leaps onto the couch. Tana groans, but I laugh because it's Ryan.

He pats the cushion, and Tana shyly sits next to him. I join her, and then Zane slides in next to me. All the other students file in, taking chairs and the other, less comfortable couch and sitting on the rug in front.

Ryan leans over and says, "LCA was supposed to

construct an actual movie theater, but the project got halted last year."

Now that I know about Ryan's brother William, I realize that's probably how Ryan gets his info. Maybe alumni get a newsletter or something.

"Oh, this is that kaiju movie I heard about," I say, glancing at the flyer on the wall. "Didn't this just come out?"

"One of the donors is a movie executive," Ryan explains. "Nice perk, right?"

"Definitely," Tana says.

The lights dim, and everyone gets quiet as the movie starts.

This is a movie I would have seen with Dad. He loves all those old Ultraman and Godzilla movies. Neither of us has been to the movie theater in years, first because of the pandemic and then because Mom died.

I want to do fun things with Dad. I want to be home with Dad.

When the credits roll and the lights come back up, Zane's head is lolled back and he's sleeping!

"How could he sleep through that?" Tana asks. "It was action-packed!"

"He can sleep anywhere," Ryan says, laughing. He stands up and then shakes his roommate. Zane starts awake, looking alarmed, but when he sees Ryan, he relaxes.

"Sweet dreams," Ryan says to us as they leave the room.

But those sweet dreams don't come right away. Back in the room, I have a hard time falling asleep. I pull the blankets up, but then feel overheated and kick the covers off. I expect Tana to tell me to stop making so much noise. Then Sir Grey meows. He rarely makes any sounds. I glance at my clock. One a.m. I groan.

At least it's the weekend. I close my eyes, but Sir Grey meows again. I sit up at the same time Tana turns on her flashlight. There in the beam of light is Sir Grey sitting at the door, staring at two silver envelopes. He skitters away with an annoyed hiss when Tana and I both pounce on the envelopes.

We take our prizes to our usual spot on the floor between our beds, facing each other. It's cloudy out and pitch-dark, so I wait my turn to use Tana's flashlight. I watch her face as she reads her card. Her eyes widen in surprise.

She hands me the flashlight and returns to her bed, tucking her envelope under her pillow. I slide my fingers under the flap to unseal it, pull out the now familiar charcoal-colored card, and turn on the flashlight to read.

Meg Mizuno,
Congratulations on making it this far.
The final envelope leads to how to claim the prize.

*Find it by the Monday after Thanksgiving
break, or the treasure hunt is off.
Only the BEST of the BEST can win.
Prove yourself or disappear.
Sometimes the clue is right under your nose.
~The Mastermind*

That's it? How can that be the entire clue? I set Tana's flashlight on her nightstand and climb back into bed. I want to figure out the clue, but against my will my eyelids grow heavy, and I drift off to sleep.

CHAPTER 42

WHEN I WAKE UP, I check my watch. It's ten o'clock. It's way too silent and dark. I raise my head, and sure enough, Tana's bed is neatly made. She's undoubtedly trying to figure out the newest clue.

Sir Grey is curled up on my pillow next to my head. I listen. It's quieter than usual, like the room is muffled. Like . . . snow.

I bolt up to look out the window. It's frosted, and the outdoors is blanketed in white. Huge fluffy flakes drift in the gray sky. The first real snowfall. My heart lifts and I feel giddy. I change quickly into my uniform, tugging on woolen LCA-approved leggings and my black snow boots, and bundle up in my down coat.

I head outside to the front of the manor, breathing in

the fresh chilled air. I've always loved the first snowfall. As I turn the corner, I get smacked in the face with a snowball. I screech and rub my face with my mittened hands. Ryan watches me from a distance, a grin on his face and another snowball in his hand.

"You're dead!" I shout.

He takes off running, but I'm not new to this. I quickly scoop snow into hard-packed balls and nail the back of his head. He turns, his face full of delighted surprise. He raises his hand, holding a snowball. I yelp and dive behind one of the many statues on the grounds. But another snowball beans me from behind.

When I turn to see Winsome, I'm surprised, but undeterred. I pivot and throw my next snowball. But she's quick and I miss. She takes off running into the woods, laughter bubbling up from her as she goes.

I peek back out from behind the statue, and a snowball whooshes dangerously close past my face.

"Almost got you!" Ryan cackles.

But before he can finish laughing, I throw a snowball right into his face. He starts coughing while swiping at his eyes with his gloved hands.

"You okay?" I ask, by his side in an instant. I feel bad for hitting him so hard.

He reacts by taking an armful of snow and dumping it over my head.

"Hey!" I shout. "Foul! I was checking on you out of concern."

He laughs, brushing snow off my shoulders. "Fine. Let's partner up. The eighth years made a fort, and I want to take it over."

I glance over to where Ryan points. Walls of snow provide cover as snowballs fly over at a group of students taking refuge by the benches. I hear shouts, cheers, and a few curses. And laughter. So much laughter. It feels right that the first snow is mixed with joy. The laughter reminds me of another first snowfall.

"Megumi! Wake up!" Mom nudged me.

I groaned. Even at the age of seven, I was not a morning person.

"It snowed last night," Mom said. "Come on!"

Mom was fully dressed in her long down coat and a multicolored knit cap pulled down over her ears. Her eyes danced.

She bundled me up and we stepped into the backyard, where Dad was waiting with a smile. And then he pelted me with a snowball. Mom grabbed me and pulled me behind a bush, and we stocked up with our own snowballs. And it was on! Me and Mom against Dad. That became a tradition. First snowfall, first snowball fight. That tradition lasted until Mom died.

By the first snowfall without Mom, I'd already been

forced to move to Aunt Vivian's. Dad was away on another business trip. I silently ate cereal for breakfast, and then Aunt Vivian drove me to school, complaining the entire way about how much she hated driving in the snow and how she'd never had to do that before I came to live with her. That was the first day I cut class.

At least this memory doesn't make me cry. This time the memory fills me with determination, and I harden my resolve. I'm going to win this treasure hunt.

"Aren't you going to look for the next envelope?" I ask Ryan.

He blows out breath, and a puff of steam escapes his lips. "I can't figure out what it means. Besides, we need some fun. Come on, Meg!"

He takes off toward the fort, but I return to the manor. The happy voices fade behind me, and I hurry to my room. Tana's not there. I didn't see her or Zane outside. Either of them could have already solved the clue on the card. Either of them could already have that envelope.

Sir Grey greets me with a soft chirp and rubs against my legs. I try not to trip over him while I peel off my damp layers. I grab the clue card and read it for the hundredth time, hoping something will leap out at me. I try rearranging words and then letters. Nope. There are no numbers mentioned and there is no obvious cipher. I try underlining every other word. Nothing. Frustration builds in me. I pace the room, getting dizzy. Sir Grey leaps onto my bed to watch me with wary eyes.

Think, think, think, Megumi!

What if Tana has already figured this out? Did her computer skills help her decipher this? I read the clue yet again. The line "Prove yourself or disappear" seems oddly threatening. If only I could disappear and be invisible, then I could follow Tana and see what she comes up with on the computer.

Wait a minute.

A grin bursts onto my face. I've got it!

CHAPTER 43

THERE IS A STRANGE wide empty space on the bottom half of the clue card. My wishing to be invisible reminds me of the time when Mom used invisible ink on a treasure hunt clue.

I tuck the card into my backpack. I have a couple of hours until roll call at gym. I know where to go, thanks to that conversation I had with Ryan about why his shirts are so crisp. My cheeks warm as I recall that Ryan thought I was checking him out, when really, I'm just observant. And my face gets warmer still when I think of the joy on his face when I hit him with the snowball, and how much fun it was hanging out with him. *Focus, Megumi!*

I head for the stairwell at the back of the manor,

away from Colette's room. She's been absent from my orbit since handing me the Halloween party detention. It makes me nervous, like she's plotting something big to get me kicked out.

I go down two flights of stairs to the basement, where I've never been. I follow the signs to the laundry room. It's the least fancy room I've seen here at LCA, with concrete floors and no windows. The fluorescent lights hum. The three washing machines and two dryers are empty and silent, but that's not why I'm here.

I scan the room and find what I'm looking for. I stride over to the ironing board and slap the clue card onto it. The iron is on a shelf with boxes of detergent pods and dryer sheets. I plug the iron in, turning it to medium setting. After the iron warms up, I slowly run it across the clue card.

Words appear, just as I hoped. But before I can read them, I hear voices. Not wanting to get caught, I tuck the card back into my backpack, put everything away, and hurry to the one place where I know none of the other three will find me. I promised never to return there, but I'll risk Jung's wrath in order not to give anything away to my competition. I don't want to risk that Zane will return to the other secret room while I'm there with this clue.

I knock once on the panel just in case Jung is in her secret room. No answer. My heart pounds as I open the wall. She's not here. I step in and close the panel behind me to read the card.

The letters are written with care and are easy to read.

You've known what to do from the first.

I know where the envelope is.

CHAPTER 44

THE KEY WORDS ARE "the first." The first envelope we had to find was in the staff library. The next envelope is there, and probably in the same book. The question is, How am I going to break into the library alone? Because I need to do this on my own. There's only one envelope, and teaming up with others won't work anymore.

I hoped to spend gym pondering my options, but LCA takes full advantage of the snow. We're sent off in small groups to snowshoe. As I huff and puff, trying to snowshoe across the fields near the manor, I can't think straight because it takes all my energy and brain to not fall over. Although, maybe if I fell over and just lay there, I'd be left alone.

"Move it, Mizuno," Arianna Hernandez, twelfth-year student and one of the TAs, shouts at me from the front of the line.

So I do.

By dinner I still don't have a plan.

"Have any of you figured out the clue?" Ryan asks at dinner.

Rather than attempt to lie, I shove a big spoonful of fried rice into my mouth. I chew exaggeratedly and slowly, making a show of not being able to answer while my mind spins.

"Meg," Tana says in a disappointed tone.

I make a *Who me?* face and keep chewing.

"Ah, Meg is getting competitive," Ryan says, waggling his eyebrows up and down. It's comical and adorable at the same time.

I swallow my food so I can respond. "Hey, I've always been competitive."

"No," Tana says. "You told me about the first clue."

"She told you and Zane," Ryan says with an injured look. He puts his hand to his heart.

"I told you right after," I say, rolling my eyes.

"Snitch," Zane says.

We all shut up, but when we look at Zane, he's smiling just a tiny bit.

"What about you?" I ask Zane.

"What about me?"

"How did you find the tiny treasure chest without the clue on the key?" I ask.

"I was searching in the library and came across the

treasure chest and broke in," he says as if he figured it out all on his own.

"Because *I* gave you that clue," I say to remind him.

Zane shrugs.

"And how did Ryan find his item?" I prod, raising my eyebrows at him.

Ryan laughs and says, "No idea about a key, but yeah, Zane showed me the treasure chest and broke in so I could get my item."

Zane rolls his eyes at my satisfied smile. If not for the three of us, Ryan probably wouldn't still be in this race.

"Does this mean none of us has figured out the latest clue?" Tana asks.

"It at least means *you* haven't figure it out," Ryan says with a smirk.

Suddenly Colette is next to me, leaning a hand on the table. "Meg, come see me in my room."

She walks away, her posture too confident.

"Now what?" I mumble.

When I get to Colette's room, she opens the door before I knock. She waves me in, closes the door, and once again points me to the desk.

There's something on it. What I see nearly makes my heart stop.

CHAPTER 45

IT'S THE LITTLE TREASURE chest from the library. Did Colette overhear us at dinner? No, she couldn't have. I school my face to hide my shock, glad my back is to Colette. When I turn to her, I channel Ryan and ask in a sweet voice, "Is this for me?"

Colette glares. "What is it?"

I walk over to it and lift the lid. Five items remain. "It looks like a treasure chest." I'm proud of myself for not giving anything away, but I know that the longer I stay here the more I risk inadvertently revealing something to her.

"Don't be smart," Colette snaps. "What's it for?"

I don't have to pretend to be annoyed, because I am. If she figures this out, the treasure hunt and my chance for the prize disappear. "How am I supposed to know?"

"You're telling me you don't know anything about this? Why was this hidden behind books in the library? The same library that students were flocking to earlier in the semester." Colette's voice gets shrill.

Wow. She seriously hates being left out.

"I know nothing." I cross my arms. "I have to get ready for Saturday evening activity. Unless you're telling me I'm excused from attending?"

She lets me go, but I know it's not the end. If I were her, I'd start snooping or pressuring other students. I can't be the only one she's harassing. Someone might cave. Anyone not left in the game might tell Colette something, even if they don't mean to. I really have to find that envelope quicker than ever, before Colette ruins it.

On my way to the Green Room, I peer down the staff hall. I can get to the staff library, but I can't get in without help. I have to figure out a way.

It's game night. Board games are stacked everywhere, and students join whatever game they're most interested in. I don't have any favorites. I'm glad when Tana waves me over to a small table in the back of the room, where she sits with Ryan and Zane. She's got a board game set up with colored pieces and dice. When I sit down, all three lean in as Ryan asks, "What did Colette want?"

When I tell them about the treasure chest, Zane

shakes his head. "Why did the Mastermind leave it? That seems sloppy, when they're the one saying don't get caught."

I shrug. "Maybe something happened that kept them from removing it."

"Who could it be?" Zane asks. "It has to be someone on campus. Not a teacher, but it can't be a student, either."

"It doesn't matter," Ryan says.

Zane cocks his head at his roommate. "Doesn't it? What's the point of this whole game? It can't be just out of generosity."

"Could be," Ryan counters. "Some rich donor could have offered a prize, and maybe Dr. Ward is running the game."

I think about that ledger and the dollar amounts getting smaller, and I recall the conversation I overheard, when Dr. Ward was insisting on getting more money for the school. I doubt that she is involved in giving away money to students. But I keep that to myself.

"Are you going to tell us what the clue is, Meg?" Ryan asks in a very sweet voice.

"That trick doesn't work on me," I say, flashing him an equally sweet smile.

Zane actually laughs as Ryan frowns.

The noise level suddenly drops, and I turn to see Colette standing in the doorway. The four of us focus on our game, dropping all conversation about the treasure hunt.

Ryan groans as Tana sends one of his pieces right back to the beginning for the third time.

"Sorry!" she says with a bit too much glee.

"Why are you picking on me?" Ryan asks. "You should be focusing on your evil roommate."

"Evil?" I mock-gasp. "Me?"

"Tell us what you know," Ryan says. "We all know you've figured it out."

I ignore him, smiling to myself.

By ten o'clock Tana has won the third game in a row. I stand and stretch. The room has emptied out, with only a handful of students still playing other games.

"Room check in thirty minutes," I say.

"One more round," Ryan says. "I have to beat Tana."

"Good luck with that," I say. "I'm tired. I'm going to head back. Tana?"

She smiles, a faint blush to her cheeks. "I think I'll beat Ryan one more time."

Zane stands too. "I'm done. See you two later."

We walk out of the room together.

"I'll figure it out, Mizuno," he says at the stairwell where we'll go in opposite directions to our dorm rooms.

"You probably will, Yoshikawa."

As I walk to the girls' wing, I'm surprised at how

relaxed I feel. It's apparent that Tana and the others intend to win. I would have expected to feel more ruthless.

When I get to my room, I pat my pocket and curse in Japanese. I've locked myself out for the first time. I've been so distracted by this treasure hunt. Good thing I know where my roommate is.

I head back to the Green Room, and as I approach, I hear Tana and Ryan talking.

"We could hypnotize her, make her reveal the answer," Ryan says.

Tana laughs. "Or mix a magic potion. A truth serum!"

"Better yet, why don't we ransack your room?" Ryan asks so softly that I need to lean in to hear. "I mean, you have access to it! I'm sure she's written down the answer somewhere."

My heart hammers. Are they talking about me? Stealing from me?

There's a brief silence before Tana answers. "Right, I'll wait till she's out of the room and dig around for the card. She probably wrote the answer on it."

"You and me, Tana. We make a good team. We'll get that prize from Meg no matter what!"

I'm proud that I manage to back away silently, instead of falling over in shock. I scurry to the girls' wing, cursing myself. I shouldn't be surprised. Not at all! This is what I knew would happen if I let anyone in, if I fooled myself into thinking friends were real. Tana said I could trust her. She said she'd never betray me. She said she'd win fair. But they were lies!

I knock on Colette's door and accept a demerit for forgetting my room key. I'd much rather get a demerit than ask Tana for anything ever again.

CHAPTER 46

I MANAGE TO DODGE everyone, including Tana, all day on Sunday, and then eat very quickly at dinner and don't say a word. I'm mad at myself for making such a big mistake by actually trusting Tana, Ryan, and even Zane. Feeling like we might be friends made me lose my razor-sharp focus. I should have learned my lesson from Addy. No more being weak. They are my classmates and nothing more.

I avoid my room as much as possible, cutting it close before curfew check and promptly going to sleep right after.

Monday morning at breakfast, all three are at the table before me.

"Where were you yesterday?" Tana asks with a smile. "Or have you already found the envelope?"

"Tana!" Ryan chastises her. "Now you've given it away that you don't have it."

"Well, you don't either, then!"

She and Ryan grin at each other. Because they're a team now.

"Meg?" Ryan asks, flashing that too-pretty smile at me. The one he uses to trick people into liking him.

"If you think I'm telling you all anything, you're mistaken," I say sharply.

In a flash I notice Tana's hurt feelings, Ryan's surprise, and Zane's zero reaction. Tana and Ryan are great actors.

The stakes are even higher now, because while I still want to win the prize, more than ever I want to get out of here. I don't belong at LCA. I could do perfectly well in a public school if only Dad would let me move home.

Ryan puts his elbows on the table, leaning toward me. "I know you've figured out the clue, Meg. Come on and be a sport and let us in on it. Or at least give us a hint."

Or he and Tana will search my side of the room for clues. Too bad for them, because I am now carrying my clue card with me.

"If you were as smart as your brother, you'd figure it out on your own, but we all know that the only reason you're still in this is because you use others to do the work for you. You don't deserve to win," I say.

Tana gasps.

"Wow," Ryan says, his voice going cold. "I thought we were friends."

"You thought wrong."

I get through the rest of the morning without saying another word to any of them. They, in turn, are also quiet, which is fine by me. And unlike breakfast, when they tried to chat with me, lunch is blissfully silent. I eat quickly. When I bus my dishes, Tana joins me.

"Meg, you don't have to share anything about the treasure hunt. That's totally your right. But you can still talk to us. We're still friends," she says quietly.

I look straight into her lying eyes as I dump my dish into a bin. "Let's be clear, Tana. We aren't friends."

Tana blinks quickly, and I take off to meet Carole.

"Are you okay?" Carole asks when I meet her at our bench.

"Sure," I say, forcing a smile. I still need to do well in classes.

She watches me for a few seconds, and then says, "Okay, so I have to be away again this week. I'm procuring some art for the museum. I've talked to Dr. Ward, and I'm giving you an assignment."

Oh goody.

"I want you to learn the hiking trails on the property," she says.

"Um, isn't the property, like, a million acres?"

Carole laughs. "Well, it may seem that way. Start with the blue trails by the manor. There's a trail map in the library. Those are easy and loop back around. You can't get lost. I'll see you next week!"

Oh boy, I guess it's too late to rethink my IS. Then again, Carole being away is extremely convenient. I can focus on the treasure hunt while having an excuse to be on my own every afternoon. It's like she's giving me a gift.

I need to take full advantage, because it's likely that the others will figure out the invisible ink thing. If Zane figures it out, he'll get into the staff library with no problem.

ON TUESDAY THE FOUR of us are the ideal students in class. We don't talk and we don't interact.

At the end of Ms. Sheth's Life Skills lecture, something about credit cards and debt, she leans against her desk and crosses her arms.

"Is something going on that I should know about?" she asks.

"Why do you ask?" Ryan asks, in *that* voice.

"I don't think I've ever seen the four of you this quiet or still."

Tana shuffles in her seat.

"I think we're just tired from midterms," Ryan says.

"I see." Ms. Sheth nods.

As we're packing up to leave for our science class, Ms.

Sheth calls my name. "Meg, how's the extra-credit assignment going?"

"Oh, was that mandatory?" I've been distracted by everything else.

"No, but I *am* curious to find out what happened to Leland Chase's descendants." Ms. Sheth smiles. "Aren't you?"

I feel Tana nearly vibrating next to me. She wants the extra credit. And there's no way I'm giving her anything. An idea suddenly comes to me, but I can't say anything in front of the others.

"Actually, I have been meaning to work on that," I say. "Can I stay behind and ask you something?"

"Sure." Ms. Sheth nods to the others and dismisses them.

As soon as I know we're alone, I ask, "Could I check the staff library for books?"

Ms. Sheth raises her eyebrows. "How do you know about the staff library? Anyway, students are not allowed in there. But you should be able to find something in the student library or even online. Try the computer room."

It was worth a shot. "Sure. Thanks."

When I get to Ms. Heller's room, I take my seat next to Tana, open my lab book, and get through the rest of the morning without another incident. In fact, Tana and Ryan make up for the awkward silence by being extra chatty in the rest of our classes. I hate to admit it, but it's a smart move. No need to have teachers noticing that anything is off. After another silent lunch, I head to IS feeling relief about it for the first time.

I choose the shortest and easiest trail to learn. I only need to do a trail once, and I'll commit it to memory. It takes me under half an hour to do the first trail, so for the remaining hour I just keep walking in a loop, lost in my thoughts. I can't get into the staff library alone. And the cold, hard truth is that I am now really alone.

I took the false friendships with Tana, Ryan, and Zane for granted. I got soft and careless. I came to this school with the intention of protecting myself from getting hurt again. I hoped Addy was a fluke, but this only proves that friends aren't to be trusted. The only person I can believe in is myself. An ache throbs in my chest. I miss Dad, and I really miss Mom. I miss my family and I miss home. I told myself I was okay being alone, but I'm not. I don't like it at all.

Time to win this prize. Time to go home.

CHAPTER 48

THE SILENCE BETWEEN THE four of us becomes normal by Thursday. Zane was never chatty during class anyway. Things are a little strained. Tana keeps trying to talk with me both in class and in our room, but I haven't said one more word to her.

After study hall Tana grabs her backpack and as usual heads off to the computer room. I wonder briefly if the other three have figured out the invisible ink, but I doubt it. They would definitely brag about it.

I head back to our room, getting more and more frustrated with each day that passes. I'm considering just trying Ryan's technique and walking right into the staff library and claiming I have a right to be there. But I'm too nervous to try that. The rule book states that there are consequences if we stray into prohibited areas, which includes the staff side of the manor. I'm not sure what the exact consequences are, but it's at least a demerit, surely.

Once I'm in my room alone, I breathe a sigh of relief. At least I have Sir Grey. Speaking of which, where is he? He always greets me when I come home.

"Hey, I'm back," I say softly. I drop to my knees and peek under the bed. "Hey. Sorry, little dude. I promise to pay more attention to you." As soon as I win this treasure hunt.

He's not there. I check the closet. He's not on his bed. I slide the door all the way open and start tossing my clothes out. Panic rises in me. Where is he?

"Meg? What's going on?"

Tana stands in the middle of the room, my clothes strewn all over the floor. I didn't even hear her come in.

I throw myself onto my bed, holding back tears. "I can't find Sir Grey."

"What?" Tana immediately dives to her bed, then yanks her covers off. She opens her closet door, but no sweet gray kitty. Soon our room looks like a tornado hit it.

I pace in circles, stepping onto and over our piles of clothes. Tana sits on her unmade bed, her knees jiggling up and down. "We have to find him," she says.

"Like you care!" I snap.

Tana's mouth presses into a firm line. "Look, Meg, I

don't know what's going on and why you're freezing me out, but know one thing for sure. I love that cat too!"

I drop back down onto my bed. She may have been lying about being my friend, but she does care about Sir Grey.

"Okay, let me think," I say. How could Sir Grey have gotten out of our room? "What if Colette broke into our room and took him?"

Tana's legs go still. "No. She wouldn't."

"She's suspicious. First she got my envelope, and then she found the treasure chest. What if she broke in here to try to figure things out? And then saw Sir Grey?"

"Colette is a lot of things, but she's not a rule breaker. She wouldn't break into our room."

Our eyes catch. We've realized at the same time that we're talking to each other. It's not that I forgot why I stopped talking to her, and I definitely haven't forgiven her, but finding Sir Grey is the priority.

"I need to talk to Colette," I say.

Tana's eyes grow wide. "On purpose?"

"I have to know if she has Sir Grey." I have to get him back.

"Do you want me to go with you?"

"No," I say.

Tana flinches and then says, "I'll keep looking. And clean up."

I straighten my shoulders. Off to do battle.

CHAPTER 49

I DON'T HAVE A plan, but I knock on Colette's door anyway. It swings open, and Colette is visibly pleased to see me. Or maybe the more accurate word is "triumphant." I step into her room, and she shuts the door behind me with a firm click.

"Finally decided to play?" she asks, crossing her arms.

For a second I think she means the treasure hunt, but then I realize she means the little game of snitch that she's set up for me.

"What do I get?" I ask, stalling.

"The chance to become RA when you reach eleventh year. I'll coach you and leave a letter of recommendation for you." Colette's eyes shine.

I try to get a good look around her room without being

obvious, find some hint that Sir Grey is in here. He must be so frightened! It's true that I don't like Colette, but I never thought she was evil. Stealing pets is evil!

"That's it?" I ask. "I don't want to be RA!"

Now she frowns. "Then, what is it you want? You think I'm going to give you money? Or help you cheat to get better grades?"

I hold in a sigh. "I don't need money, and I'm doing fine in the grades department."

"Then, why are you here?"

Oops. I take a deep breath. She doesn't have Sir Grey. If she did, she would have dangled him in front of me by now.

"Why do you hate me?" This pops out of my mouth before I have a chance to stop myself. Colette and I are equally surprised.

Her mouth gapes for a long moment before her eyes go hard and she snaps her mouth shut. "Who says I hate you?"

"It feels that way."

"I don't treat you any differently than other LCA students."

I raise my eyebrows.

"I have a job. And even if everyone thinks the RA is nothing but a teacher's pet, it's an important job. I have to make sure everyone follows the rules so that no one gets hurt. I'm responsible for each of you girls."

I say nothing.

"It's an important job," Colette says. And then in almost a whisper, "I'm important."

How did I miss this? For all my bragging about how observant I am, I missed this. Colette took this job for power and control but ended up lonelier than before. She and I are the same that way, I realize. Maybe she was hurt before, and she doesn't want to risk that again.

"It *is* an important job," I say.

Colette narrows her eyes at me like I'm mocking her. But when I don't say anything else, her shoulders slump and she plops down onto her desk chair. "Nobody gets it. Everyone acts like I'm out to get them, when I'm only doing my job."

"It isn't clear," I say cautiously, afraid she's going to bite my head off. "I mean, yeah, you make sure we all get to class and follow rules, but you also kind of terrify us to the point where we avoid you."

"People are scared of me?"

I can't tell if she's upset or pleased about that. I shrug.

"*You're* not scared of me," Colette says. When I don't respond, she continues, "Everyone hates me."

"I think 'hate' is a strong word," I say. "Everyone is afraid of you because every time they see you, you yell at them. Or threaten them."

A long minute ticks by.

"Do you know why I'm here?" she asks.

"No."

"I got kicked out of my middle school for being a bully."

I'm not surprised, but I try not to show that.

"But only because otherwise everyone ignored me," she says, her voice rising defensively. "Maybe if kids were nice to me, I'd be nice back."

"Or maybe if you were nice to others, *they* would be nice back."

She gives me a suspicious look.

I raise my hands. "Not, like, let people break the rules or anything, but you know, don't be so scary about it."

Colette stands. "Speaking of rules, it's time for dinner. Last chance. Are you sure there's nothing you want to tell me?"

I have to give her points for persistence. "There's nothing going on." That is an outright lie, but I still have my priorities. Find Sir Grey. Win the treasure hunt. And she can't help me do either.

I hurry back to my room, hoping Tana found our kitty.

When I step in, the room is as neat as it ever is, but it's obvious from the look on Tana's face that she was hoping I was coming back with Sir Grey.

We are now both officially panicked.

CHAPTER 50

WE MUST LOOK PRETTY upset, because the first thing Ryan says when Tana and I sit down for dinner is, "What's wrong?"

Tana glances at me. I look down at my place setting, pondering. She's asking for permission to tell the guys, but I don't want to. I don't trust them. I don't trust anyone.

Tana nudges my arm gently. I sigh. When I look up at Ryan and Zane, Ryan narrows his eyes at me.

"Wait," he says, turning back to Tana. "*You're* okay, Tana? There's something wrong with her?"

He says "her" in an icy tone, and that he won't even say my name shows how much I hurt him with my comments the other day. One thing I've learned about Ryan is that he's a people pleaser. I know I've really hurt him because he's not flashing that smile at me, trying to warm me up. Did he deserve it? Yes. He's the one who was trying to betray me. So why does it bother me that it's obvious he's angry with me?

But the real issue here isn't that. Sir Grey is missing. No matter how upset Ryan is, I don't think he'd get me in trouble by spilling my secret. I exchange looks with Tana. Our secret. Jung is the only one other than Tana who knows about Sir Grey. Dare I share with two more people?

I think of Sir Grey, lost in this big manor. What if a teacher finds him? I'd never see him again!

Leaning forward to Ryan and Zane, I whisper, "Tana and I have a pet cat. He's missing."

"What can we do to help?" Ryan asks without missing a beat. He's probably jumping in to help Tana, since I mentioned that the cat belongs to both of us, but that's fine with me.

"Where have you looked?" Zane asks.

"He's not in our room, and I'm almost positive I didn't leave our door open," Tana says. "Meg checked in with Colette, and she doesn't have him."

"We can look around the manor," Ryan says.

Even though Ryan has every right to hold back, to be mad at me, he doesn't hesitate. They are all in, willing to help. They have nothing to gain by pretending to help. At least not that I can see. I don't entirely trust my own judgment anymore. I don't forgive him or Tana, but again, the priority is finding Sir Grey.

"It will go faster if we tell others so they can help," Ryan continues. Now he gives me a hard look. "Just because you rely on your friends to help doesn't mean you're using them."

Ah. So he isn't going to let my comment go. That's fine, because I'm not going to let it go that he tried to betray me.

Ryan shrugs. "Also, you know we don't snitch on one another. We don't have to tell everyone. There are friends we trust, right?"

Friends. I don't have those anymore. Friends can hurt you. Ryan, Zane, and Tana watch me, waiting for me to make the decision. Trust is hard to come by, but finding Sir Grey is more important. Because losing him would break my heart. It seems that no matter what I do to try to protect myself, I can still get hurt.

"Okay," I say. "We need to find him quickly."

"You can trust me," Winsome says from my right.

I raise my eyebrows at her. "Because you eavesdrop?"

She flashes a smile. "Can't blame a girl for being curious. You all are whispering like thieves."

"You can help? *And* keep it quiet?" I ask.

"I'll get the word out," she says. "But you sure like to test boundaries."

"It is a weakness," I admit.

"Nah. I respect that," Winsome says, surprising me.

Dinner is served, and the conversation volume rises. The news is traveling down the table. I eat quickly but freeze when a chair screeches against the floor. Colette strides to the front of the room. Has the news gotten to her?

She clears her throat. "With permission from Dr. Ward," she says, "I have decided to clear everyone's record. Any demerits accumulated so far this month have been erased."

There is a moment of stunned silence. Colette walks across the room but stops at the door when students burst into cheers and applause. I see the small smile on her face as she leaves.

Everyone starts to clear their dishes at the end of the dinner hour. Before I can stand, I feel a tap on my shoulder. It's Ingrid Jensen, an eighth year and our next-door neighbor.

She smiles shyly and says, "I think something that belongs to you found its way into our room."

CHAPTER 51

SIR GREY IS SO happy to be back home that he keeps winding around and between my legs. He's purring so loudly, he's like a jet engine. Tana moves things out of her closet. The only way Sir Grey could have ended up in Ingrid and Kylie's room is if there's a hole in Tana's closet. Right now Ingrid and Kylie are tearing apart Kylie's closet.

"Found it!" Tana exclaims, her voice muffled by the coats hanging above her head.

I crawl into her closet with her, and in the far back corner is a hole just big enough for a small cat to squeeze through. Tana squeals as a hand pokes through. Kylie laughs and pulls her hand back to her side. Tana places a box to block the hole, and she promises to keep her closet closed.

Moments later there's a knock at the door. I let Ingrid

and Kylie into our room. Sir Grey leaps onto my bed and keeps an eye on the guests. Kylie crouches in front of him, making clicking noises, but he's not having any of it. He retreats to his bed in my closet.

Kylie stands and faces me with a sheepish smile. "I can't really blame him. This is home. I'm glad we figured it out."

Ingrid laughs. "We were blaming each other for sneaking in a pet. I'm so glad you got the word out. Neither of us wanted the responsibility, but we didn't want to kick him out either."

"But," Kylie says, looking longingly at my closet, "maybe we can visit him? Or if you ever need a cat-sitter?"

"Yeah, sure," I say.

"Colette can't know," Tana says.

Kylie laughs. "Obviously."

After they leave, I try to coax Sir Grey out of my closet, but he's had enough activity and adventure. He yawns and settles in for a nap.

"I'm glad he's back," Tana says quietly. She's sitting on her desk chair facing me. Her hands are clasped tightly in her lap. She's nervous. "Meg, I want to know what happened to make you stop talking to us. To me. I thought we were friends."

I had zero intention of talking to her about this, but her words break me, and I have to force myself not to shout. "I thought we were friends too, but you proved me wrong." My voice is a harsh whisper, like sandpaper.

Her eyes grow wide. "How? What did I do?"

"You know exactly what you did!" I grab my pillow and squeeze it.

"I don't, Meg! Tell me, please!"

I glare at her. "You said you'd never betray me. You said I could trust you."

"You *can* trust me. I wouldn't ever betray you, Meg. I promise!"

"Stop!" This time I do shout, and Tana flinches. I lower my voice. "Don't make promises you can't keep."

Tana grabs a tissue from her desk and wipes her eyes. "I really have no idea what you're talking about."

"You and Ryan are conspiring against me, planning to cheat to win!"

"What? No! Meg! I would never!"

"Don't lie to me. I heard you! I heard both of you!"

Tana stands up in frustration, fists by her sides. "When? When would you have heard this imaginary conversation?"

"On game night!" I shout again. I take a deep breath and continue, "I left to go to our room, but I'd forgotten my key in the room. When I went back to borrow your key, I heard the two of you talking about ransacking the room to find my clue card!"

Tana's face goes from stony to confused, and then I see the moment she realizes she's busted. I want to feel triumphant, but instead I have to do everything I can not to cry.

"Oh, Meg," Tana says, sitting back down in her chair, her shoulders slumped. "You're wrong. I mean, you heard right, but you don't have the full context."

"What kind of context do I need? I heard what I heard."

Tana's cheeks get pink.

"What?" I ask.

"Um, after you and Zane left, Ryan and I were, um, teasing each other. You know, joking around." The rest of Tana's face now matches her pink cheeks.

I cock my head at her. "You mean *flirting?*"

Now Tana's face goes magenta, and if we were still friends, I'd give her a hard time about this. But I don't care. I don't.

"Okay, yeah, maybe flirting. But it's *Ryan*, so I know it doesn't mean anything," she says. "We were going on about how we knew you had figured out the clue card, and we were joking about how we'd get you to spill. Like, hypnosis or a magic potion."

I do recall them saying that.

"And okay, Ryan did say that thing about ransacking our room, but he was smiling when he said it, and then I was caught up in the conversation and riffed off him. But, Meg, you must have heard what I said a few seconds after."

I shake my head slowly. "I left after you said you two would team up against me."

She cringes. "I totally get why you're upset, Meg, but I wish you'd heard the rest of it. I told Ryan I would never cheat, and I would never betray you. And Ryan agreed and said he was kidding and that he wouldn't betray any of us."

I waver. I really want to believe her. I hug my pillow tighter and bury my face in it. A few seconds later I feel Tana sit down on the bed next to me. She rests her hand on my shoulder, tentatively, and when I don't react, she reaches around me for a full-fledged hug.

"Megumi Mizuno," she says in a whisper against my shoulder, "I would never hurt you, but especially after you shared that story about your former best friend. I promise you, I'm your friend. Forever. No matter what."

I finally lift my face from my pillow and duck out of her arms. I scoot back on my bed and look at her.

"I want to believe you," I say. But I don't think I can risk it. It hurts too much.

"I will regain your trust," Tana says. "I'll prove how much your friendship means to me. I'll help you win this treasure hunt."

"What?" I blink at her. "But you always have to win."

"Not always. Not when friendship is more important."

There's a rap on the door and Colette says, "Why are your lights on? Lights-out. NOW!"

We scurry to our beds, and Tana shuts off her light.

After a few long minutes she says, "Good night, Meg."

CHAPTER 52

FRIDAY NIGHT ACTIVITY IS thankfully in the kitchen, because I'm not sure I could take going back to the Green Room. Even after her explanation, I'm treading carefully with Tana. I haven't made up with Ryan, but I suppose I'll have to deal with him at some point.

Oliver steps to the front of the kitchen. "This evening's activity will be led by the pastry chef, Chef Maddie. We're baking the LCA favorite, snickerdoodles."

My stomach rumbles. Those are my favorite cookies, served only during weekend buffets, and they disappear fast.

I purposely choose to stand near the back, away from the other seventh years, but they join me. Zane is singularly focused on following the instructions, and Ryan is unusually silent, but Tana more than makes up for them.

"Here's your sugar, Meg," she says cheerfully.

And a minute later, "Do you want extra cinnamon, Meg?" Tana remembers that I always take the cookies with the most cinnamon.

Tana is determined to break down my defenses. By the end of the evening, most of us are dusted in flour. Zane, in fact, has so much flour in his hair that he looks like an ojiichan with gray hair. I bite back a smile.

"Glad I can amuse you, Mizuno," Zane deadpans, shaking his head and sprinkling us with flour.

"Is that a smile?" Ryan asks me.

I glance at Tana, curious whether she's the reason why Ryan is talking to me again.

She gives me a sheepish shrug. "I hated that we were fighting," she says softly.

Ryan clears his throat. "I'm sorry I said what I did. Even if I was kidding around, I shouldn't have said it, Meg," he says to me in a serious tone I don't think I've ever heard from him.

I swallow the lump in my throat (probably my pride) and say, "I'm sorry for what I said too. I don't really believe you use your friends. And you're totally better than your brother."

Ryan smiles at me. Not the one he flashes to charm others, but a real smile. Despite my efforts, my heart thaws a little.

I admit it. This is way nicer than being alone. This is way nicer than being friendless. Do I trust them 100 percent? No. But we four have come this far in the treasure hunt because we teamed up. Out of necessity? Perhaps. But the truth is, I was having fun sharing the thrill of solving the clues, and the mild competition between us all. I hadn't had real fun since before Mom died.

Here's the truth. I need to win. I can't get the next envelope alone. If one of us doesn't find the prize, nobody wins. Better to be in the running than to have the game end with no winner. And what better way to test Tana's claim of friendship?

I make up my mind.

CHAPTER 53

THE NEXT DAY, I surprise Tana, Ryan, and Zane by showing up at Saturday breakfast.

"Wow," Ryan says. "This is a first."

I frown. "I get up in the mornings when I have to."

Tana jumps in. "We're just happy to see you, Meg."

It's nice that we're talking again, but that doesn't mean I trust them 100 percent. I still want to win.

"Okay, you all were right," I say, leaning forward over my cereal bowl. "I did figure out the clue. And I can't get to the next one without your help."

"You gave Ryan a hard time, saying that he uses people," Zane says, his voice colder than usual. "Now you want to use us."

Tana cuts her eyes to him, like she's annoyed with him. "Of course we'll help, Meg!"

Wow. Zane is more protective of Ryan than I gave him credit for. Maybe friendships can be real.

"I apologized to Ryan," I say. "And we've all been working together throughout the game, off and on."

"So, you're making a deal with us?" Ryan asks cautiously.

I shake my head. "Zane's right. Nothing is free. We all want to win. I don't expect favors."

Zane's mouth curves into a self-righteous smile.

"I'll tell you what the clue is," I say. "We work together to get the next envelope, and we'll figure out next steps."

Ryan tilts his chair back. "Okay," he drawls. "I'm in."

"How do you know we won't just go solo after you tell us the clue?" Zane asks me.

I shrug. "I don't, but one of us needs to find it by the Monday after Thanksgiving, or no one wins."

Ryan brings down the front legs of his chair with a loud thunk. "We're a team."

Are we, though?

"Lay it on us," Ryan says.

"The clue is under your nose," I say. "It's invisible ink."

"That's a thing?" Ryan asks. "That sounds like something in a spy novel."

"Wow," Tana says. "That's brilliant! You figured it out, Meg. I don't think I would have ever thought of that. I was putting all the letters into a computer program, but nothing was making sense."

"What did it say?" Zane asks.

"You've known what to do from the first," I say. I pause, seeing if anyone gets it.

Barely a second passes before Tana exclaims, "The first location! We need to get back to the staff library!"

It's a good thing she didn't figure out the invisible ink thing, or she would have probably already won by now.

I turn to Ryan. "How did you get the envelope in the staff library?"

Ryan tilts his chair back again. "No thanks to you three."

"Hey," I say. "I ended up telling you where it was."

"I waltzed right in." Ryan grins.

"Of course you did," I say.

"You walked into the staff library?" Tana says with disbelief. "No one stopped you?"

"I ran into the cleaning crew," Ryan says. "I told them I was on an errand."

"And they believed you?" I ask.

"You're surprised?" Zane counters.

No. I guess I'm not.

"That's not going to work a second time," Tana says.

"Probably not," Ryan agrees, setting his chair back down on four legs.

Plus, there's no way I trust him on his own. He could get the envelope, read it, and go on to win. It's still a competition.

"I'll go," Zane says. "I can break in after lights-out."

"No way," I say.

"Okay, then, Mizuno. What's your brilliant plan?"

"We do this together," I say. "As a group. We take the risk together."

And we all keep an eye on one another.

CHAPTER 54

THE PLAN IS SIMPLE. It has to be. There are too many possible obstacles and things that can go wrong. The best thing is to repeat a previous success. There's no way the three of us can wander the staff side together with Ryan. I don't care how charming he is. He won't be able to convince anyone that the four of us are not up to any trouble. So, it's back to Zane and his lock-picking.

We wait for lights-out in our respective rooms. Trying to sneak out during movie night would be too risky.

After lights-out Tana and I wait thirty minutes, as we all agreed. We don't want to risk an RA hearing us. Colette has gotten noticeably more chill, but that doesn't mean she won't hand out demerits for real rules being broken. We would be breaking several tonight. I can't deny the rush I feel every time I solve a clue. For me the risk is worth it. For the prize and for the thrill.

It feels good to tug on my faded black jeans and my favorite black hoodie. I hand Tana one of my black sweatshirts, and we exchange a smile. Things are feeling more like before, like we are roommates and friends. I tamp down the anxiety. I'm tired of feeling alone.

"Ready?" I ask Tana.

She pulls the sweatshirt on over her lavender long-sleeve tee. "Ready."

We walk slowly and quietly down the hall, hoping not to run into anyone. We're not in our pj's, so the going-to-the-bathroom excuse won't work.

Ryan and Zane are waiting for us when we make it to the staff side of the manor. My heart stupidly flips when I see both boys dressed in head-to-toe black. It looks like a second skin on Zane, but this is the first time I've seen Ryan in street clothes. He always wears his LCA uniform or gym clothes. If he looked good in his uniform, he looks even more like a fashion model in black pants paired with a formfitting black turtleneck. I tear my eyes away from him, forcing my mind back to the task.

The halls are dark, barely illuminated by safety lights. When we get to the staff library door, Zane lifts a finger, and we wait nervously as he continues to the end of the hall. In the dim light he waves to us. He's found a nook, an empty alcove that dead-ends at a narrow shelf, providing just enough room for the three of us to hide in while Zane picks the lock.

We don't talk. We don't whisper. We vowed not to make any unnecessary sounds, but Tana is so full of anxiety, she's breathing fast and heavy. She's so stressed that she won't even watch Zane. She's tucked behind me as Ryan and I peek out at Zane. We are touching. Ryan's chest leans against my shoulder. He is warm. Solid.

In seconds Zane has the door open. He disappears into the library. We remain frozen, waiting, barely breathing (except for Tana, who is breathing loudly enough for all of us). I shoot her a warning look, and she shrugs helplessly.

Ryan taps my shoulder, and I turn in time to see Zane stepping back into the hall, tucking the book under his jacket. Just as Zane closes the door, a light flashes onto him and a voice rings out.

"Stop right there!"

CHAPTER 55

OH MY GOD, OH my god, oh my god. Firm footsteps echo in the hall. I can't see what's happening because now I've ducked back into the alcove. We're clinging to each other as if that will help Zane disappear.

"What are you doing here, Mr. Yoshikawa?" The voice echoes down the hall.

This is not good. He's been identified. I'm panicking. In that brief second I realize that I'm not freaking out because of the treasure hunt. I'm worried for Zane. We can't let him take the fall for this on his own. But before I can come up with a rescue idea, Ryan strides out to them, making both Tana and me gasp quietly.

"There you are," Ryan says.

I don't dare take a peek. I couldn't if I wanted to, since

Tana has an iron grip on my arm. I lean forward, trying to hear clearly.

"Mr. Hsieh, what are you doing out of your room and on this side of the manor?"

I still can't place the voice, but it's someone who knows the students well. A person who would be able to identify me and Tana.

"Hey, Miss Jillian," Ryan says, all friendly like he's an invited guest at a party.

Oh no. Security. We are dead.

Miss Jillian answers, "Do not act like this is normal, Mr. Hsieh. Why are you both here?"

"Zane sleepwalks," Ryan says. "I noticed he was missing, so I went looking for him. He really wanders."

I blink. Brilliant! Especially since Zane hasn't said a word yet.

"Is this in his record?" Miss Jillian does not sound convinced. "This could be dangerous. He could get hurt."

"Oh, he doesn't want anyone to know, except for me. Pride," Ryan whispers.

"It's also about safety, Mr. Hsieh."

"I know, Miss Jillian. You're right. I'll talk to him about it."

"I'll escort you to your room," she says. "Is he still sleeping?"

"Yeah, I'll guide him."

"Let's go. I'll let this slide once, but you really need to let the school know."

"Thanks, Miss Jillian. I will."

I hear footsteps receding. Tana and I slump down to the floor in relief. If it had been Mrs. Jackson or any of the other, veteran security staff, it could have gone very badly. Thank goodness it was newbie and nice Miss Jillian who was on rounds tonight.

"Now what?" Tana asks, finally releasing her grip on me.

I shake my arm out. "We go back to our room. Miss Jillian is with the guys. She'll be back to finish her rounds, so we need to go now."

My heart pounds loudly in my ears the entire journey. Tana's nearly hyperventilating when we collapse onto our beds. I close my eyes, waiting for my heart to settle into a less punishing rate.

As my heart rate slows, it hits me. I'm impressed not only by Ryan's quick thinking but also by his loyalty to Zane. He didn't hesitate for a second to leap into action to rescue his roommate and friend. It's apparent that the two of them are true friends. I look over at Tana, who is sprawled on her bed. Maybe Tana and I can be that too.

I take a deep breath in and then let it out. I'm glad Zane didn't get caught. I'm glad Ryan's charm kept Miss Jillian from reporting them. I'm glad the four of us are in this together.

It's too late for me to protect myself against making friends. It's clear that I do care after all.

CHAPTER 56

SUNDAY MORNING TANA AND I are up early. It's so early that when we walk into the dining room, it's nearly empty. But Ryan and Zane are seated with full plates. When Tana and I sit across from them with our own breakfasts, Ryan breaks into a grin.

"Eat fast," he says. "We have an envelope to open."

We eat without talking. I think most of us could have skipped breakfast and been fine, but by now we know that meals are very important to Zane. When we're done, we head to the conservatory. It's private and warmish. The temps have dropped, and it's freezing outside. But when we get there, Oliver and Mateo are cozy at a table.

We go back into the manor, searching for a safe place

where we can open the envelope together. Everywhere we go either someone is already there or it feels as if someone could walk in at any moment or overhear. I'm frustrated and impatient. Time is ticking!

"I have an idea," I say, locking eyes with Zane.

Zane keeps watch in the hall outside the state room as I lead Tana and Ryan to the wall.

"We still have to keep quiet, but we won't be interrupted, at least," I say. I run my fingers along the panel, and when I find purchase, I pull. The wall swings out. I grin at the shocked looks on Tana's and Ryan's faces.

"What is this?" Tana asks in an awed whisper.

"Hurry up," Zane calls from the doorway.

I nudge Tana and Ryan inside. Zane joins us, his hair bouncing with each stride, and I shut the wall behind us. Zane and I sit, but Ryan and Tana are busy taking in the room. Ryan peers out the window as Tana runs her hand along the interior wall.

"A secret room?" Ryan says, turning back to us. "This is awesome!"

I wonder if Jung and I are the only ones who know that there are secret rooms in this manor. And I wonder if Zane and I are the only ones who know about this one.

"Shh," I say. "It's not soundproof."

Tana and Ryan drop down to sit with us on the floor. "You both know about this," Tana says to me and Zane.

For some reason I feel a blush creep up my neck and bloom on my cheeks. I drop my eyes.

"We found it accidentally," Zane says in a way that doesn't invite more discussion.

I put my hands out, and Ryan gives me the book. I flip it open and snag the silver envelope, turning it over to see if it's still sealed. It hasn't been opened.

I glance at the faces of my maybe-friends. "Why do we want to win?" I ask.

"What kind of question is that?" Ryan asks. "Just open it."

I shake my head. "If we're friends, we trust each other. We share. No more secrets."

Tana says, "It's a fair question. I admit it's been fun playing. But why do the four of us want to win?"

"I can guess," I say.

"Try us," Ryan says with a smile.

I nod at Tana. "Tana wants to win because she likes to be first. The best."

She lifts her chin but also catches my eyes. She is still willing to help me win.

"Nothing wrong with that," I say. Then I turn to Zane. "You don't have anywhere to go to during break. It makes sense you'd like to win."

"Oh," Tana says. "I didn't even think about that. That would stink to be here all winter break."

Zane shakes his head once. "I've been in worse places. I'd be fine here."

"Are you staying for Thanksgiving?" Tana asks.

"Yeah," Zane says.

"I am too," Ryan says. He looks at me.

"Same."

"Me too," Tana says. "We can hang out!"

"Okay, Meg," Ryan says. "Why do I want to win?"

"You do have a home to go to, but you don't want to be there."

For the first time Ryan doesn't have a quick smile to flash. His eyes darken and he frowns. He wraps his arms around his knees, but he doesn't disagree.

"Meg guessed right?" Tana sounds surprised. "But why don't you want to go home? I mean, you're the Hsieh empire."

"Yeah, the empire," Ryan scoffs, his voice hard. "You know, this is a donor year."

"A what?" I ask. That seems like a big change in topic.

"Every three years LCA does a big donation drive, trying to raise funds to keep the school running," Ryan says.

"But I thought that's what tuition is for," I say. From what Dad said, this school is not inexpensive.

"That only covers part of it," Ryan explains. "If you have wealthy families sending their precious offspring here, there are high expectations to meet. That takes a lot of money."

"How do you know all this?" I ask.

Ryan leans his head back against the wall and stares at the ceiling. "I'm the fourth Hsieh and the second generation to attend LCA. My father and my two older brothers graduated from here."

"Wait," Tana says. "No offense, but there are *four* Hsiehs who got into trouble and ended up here?"

I can see where she's going with this. That's quite a reputation. I think Ryan's not going to answer, but he surprises me.

"Dad attended because his uncle was into donating to educational organizations, and his uncle liked what this school offered. He wanted one of the family to attend to be sure the money was being well spent. So Dad enrolled, and then after that he became a donor. My eldest brother, Benjamin, went for the same reason Dad went, to keep an eye on things. William got caught taking a test for a classmate for money. Dad praised his entrepreneurial spirit, but when Will got caught a second time, he was sent here."

"And you?" I ask.

"Me? I belong here," Ryan says.

"That's not an answer," I say. "Your brother said something about not skating by and bringing shame onto the Hsieh empire." I remember that brief encounter when William was a guest speaker during an assembly.

"What Will said is true. You all know me by now.

Things come to me easily." Ryan shrugs. When none of us says anything else, he sighs. "The Hsieh empire." He says it like a curse. "We three sons are expected to take over. Benjamin's a lawyer, heads up the legal department. Will with his MBA and success with his new business will undoubtedly take over as Dad's heir."

"And you?" I ask.

"I like the arts," Ryan says softly, as if confessing something shameful. "I like writing fantasy and I love studying art."

"That's awesome," Tana says.

"It is, but again, why are you at LCA?" I prod.

"The arts are a fine hobby and it's great to be cultured, but it is not an acceptable path," Ryan says in a haughty tone that I can only assume is an imitation of his father.

"That's why you're here?" I ask.

Ryan nods. "Leland Chase Academy will turn you into the man you need to be," he continues in that voice. "Don't expect to return home until you've chosen an acceptable path." He shrugs again. "I wish my reason for being here was more interesting. It's embarrassing to admit that I'm here to be forced to give up things I love."

"But I thought LCA was for students who got kicked out of or didn't thrive in other schools," I say.

"Yeah," Ryan says. "For the most part, but money has a way of getting exceptions made. Plus, I'm a legacy."

"Wait. Isn't writing your IS?" I ask.

"My dad can't control everything," Ryan replies. "I want to win because this is something my dad wouldn't approve of."

Ryan's little rebellion.

"Okay," Tana interrupts, "but what happens if the school doesn't raise enough money?"

"They shut down?" Ryan says. "I don't know."

That's when I remember the ledger. "I think LCA *is* losing money."

Zane's usually stoic face shows worry. Of course. He has nowhere to go if LCA shuts down.

"If that's true, there's nothing we can do about that. So, Meg," Ryan says. "You've accurately guessed why each of us wants to play and win. Your turn."

"My mom died in the middle of my fifth-grade year, and my dad started traveling a ton for work, so I got sent to live with my aunt. I hated it there. I started doing poorly in school. Dad sent me here." I could stop there, but I don't. "My dad is selling our house early next year."

Tana gasps. "Oh, Meg!"

I blink back tears. I will not cry in front of them. "If I win this trip, Dad will be forced to spend a vacation with me. We can reconnect. I can convince him not to sell our home, our memories."

My voice breaks on the last word, and I go silent.

"Okay," Zane says in a firm voice. "We win this for Mizuno."

"What?" I ask, surprised.

"We win this for Meg," Tana says.

I notice that Ryan says nothing.

CHAPTER 57

You found what was hidden.
From ten players to one.
You're steps away from winning.
Come SNOW or ice or freezing rain,
X always marks the Spot,
but only for the best.
~The Mastermind

The silver letters are centered perfectly on the charcoal-colored card. Ryan leans over so closely, I can smell his probably very expensive shampoo. He smells like warm spices. I pass the card to him before I do something ridiculous like bury my face in his hair. He and Zane examine the card.

"It won't be invisible ink," I say. "The Mastermind won't repeat a trick."

"Let me see," Tana says, and Ryan passes it to her.

"The word 'snow' is printed a little larger than the other words," I continue, thinking out loud. "Also, the letter S in 'spot' is larger and capitalized."

"Any of these words can be a clue," Tana says, passing the card back to me.

"Could 'snow' mean we have to wait till it snows again?" Ryan ponders.

"Too obvious and also improbable," I say, shaking my head. "How can the Mastermind predict the weather?"

Ryan looks down and shrugs. I might have hurt his feelings.

"Only for the best," Tana reads out loud. "It's like the Mastermind has been trying to pit us against each other all along."

"Well, it *is* a competition," I say.

"True." Tana looks at her watch and then at Zane. "We should get going for lunch."

While we have plenty of time, we know Zane likes to get to the dining hall early. I press my ear to the wall and don't hear anything, so I open the panel and we spill out into the state room/storage room and head to the dining room.

During lunch we eat in silence as we all ponder the clue. I can't believe Zane suggested that they help me win.

I noticed that Ryan never agreed to it. I don't want to rely on Tana, either. I want to figure this out on my own.

But by Friday I haven't even come close.

It's grilled cheese and tomato soup for lunch. I'm thrilled, as it's one of my favorite cold-weather meals. Mom used to make this for me a lot.

"Meals have been going downhill," Ryan says, eyeballing his soup like it's gruel.

"It's delicious," I say, taking a second big bite of my gooey sandwich.

Zane doesn't complain. In fact, he's almost finished eating.

"Ryan does have a point, though," Tana says. "This is pretty casual and low-key for LCA if we compare it to last year's meals."

"What if the school really is in danger of shutting down?" Ryan asks.

Zane quietly sops up the rest of his soup with the crust of his sandwich. But I notice how his forehead crinkles.

"Like you said, it's not like we can do anything to help the school get more money," I say.

"Hey," Tana says in such a cheery voice, I know she's trying to keep us from getting depressed. "Since all four of us are here over Thanksgiving break, let's make sure to get all our assignments done early so we can focus on the treasure hunt."

"Sounds good," I say.

My Friday rotation assignment is shelving books in the

school library, and I'm surprised how many books there are. Hardly anyone uses this place. I'm definitely getting an arm workout. As I'm putting away the last book, a title next to it catches my eye.

History of New York Education.

I pull it out and flip to the index, and sure enough, Leland Chase Academy is listed. I turn to the given page and run my finger back and forth, skimming the words until I see a mention of this school. At first it's nothing new. It's a repetition of what Ms. Sheth told us on Founder's Day. Then my eyes catch on the word "lawsuit" and I read more carefully.

A decade after the school was taken over by a private trust, LCA successfully sued a newspaper for libel. Apparently there had been an article investigating a rumor that the school wasn't really a school but a factory to churn out executives with special skills for donor corporations. That rumor was quashed. And that's all there is about Leland Chase Academy.

No mention of what happened to Leland Chase or his family after he went bankrupt. The focus is on the school. I slide the book back onto the shelf. It wouldn't hurt to get some extra credit in Life Skills. I'm ten points behind Tana, and it would be fun to see her face if I beat her. Maybe once I win this treasure hunt, I can dig deeper.

But I have a bigger priority right now. I have until the Monday after break to find the last envelope.

CHAPTER 58

ON WEDNESDAY, IT'S COMPLETE chaos. I didn't ever think Leland Chase Academy could be in such upheaval. But apparently this is what it's like before a break.

The volume of conversation at breakfast is deafening. Ryan's eyes dance with excitement, and Zane seems impatient. Today is the last day of class before break. We get to class, and for the first time in weeks, Ms. Sheth is there before us. Her face is shining with joy. It strikes me then. She's homesick. She wants to go home. She's not so different from me.

"Good morning," Ms. Sheth sings.

"You look happy," Ryan says.

"This is our first break since the start of the school year," she says. "And I'm sure you all want to get ready. So, go ahead."

"What?" Tana asks. "We're skipping class?"

Ms. Sheth nods. "A car is coming to pick me up in less than an hour." She leans in. "I won't tell Dr. Ward if you don't."

We all leap up and assure her we won't say a word.

Her smile grows. "Have a great break and see you Monday!"

And then she's gone. If she were a cartoon, there'd be one of those little puffs of smoke in her wake, the only evidence she was here at all.

Ryan closes the door and leans onto Ms. Sheth's desk. "Zane and I figured out part of the clue."

"So have we," Tana says. "You first."

"'From ten players to one.' The numbers have to mean something," Ryan says with pride in his voice.

I glance at Zane. He, like me, figured that out already. But it looks like Zane hasn't said anything to discourage his roommate, so I won't either.

"That's great, Ryan," I say.

His smile lights up the room.

Tana jumps in. "And *we* figured that what we're looking for is outside. The clues about the weather."

Ryan nods.

Then it's quiet. That's all we have.

"Maybe we take ten steps outside?" Tana asks.

"That's still too vague," I say.

"The word 'hidden,'" Zane says. "There's a hidden room in the manor. Why not outdoors?"

"Perfect!" I exclaim. I can't believe I didn't figure that out first.

"What's our next step, Meg?" Ryan asks.

They turn to me.

"We need more information. The manor grounds are huge, and if we just wander around, we're never going to find anything," I say. "This is the final clue, so it makes sense that the Mastermind will make it challenging, but it can't be impossible."

Tana looks at her watch. "We'd better get moving. Guaranteed that Ms. Yoo won't be letting us skip language arts."

We head across the hall as I run through the clue over and over in my head.

CHAPTER 59

WE ARE ONLY HALF a dozen left on campus. The four of us, Caleb Mitchell, and Oliver. It turns out that part of an RA's responsibility is rotating for holidays. Oliver is here for Thanksgiving, so that means Colette will take much of winter break. Caleb is a twelfth year doing some sort of special study as part of his entrance requirement for a university in Spain. Nobody seems to know exactly what he's doing, but as long as he doesn't get in our way, I don't care.

None of the teachers remain, not even Dr. Ward—only the kitchen staff and the skeleton crew needed to keep LCA running because we're here. Miss Jillian has the keys to Dr. Ward's sitting room so I can have my call with Dad on Sunday. We rescheduled since he was going to be flying home from India on Saturday.

The best part about staying over a break is that we have no schedule at all. We only need to check in with Oliver at lunch and dinner. Then while he does the evening room check for the boys, Miss Jillian will do ours.

Thanksgiving meal is at two p.m., and we get to dine in one of the state rooms to seat the six of us at a round table. At each place setting of the usual china plates with the Leland Chase Academy crest is a crystal goblet filled with what I assume is sparkling cider.

Oliver lifts his glass and raises it in a toast. "Happy Thanksgiving!"

"Actually," I say, "my IS sponsor, Carole, is Ojibwe, and she told me some horrifying stories about the real Thanksgiving and the evils of colonialism."

Oliver puts his glass down and nods at me to continue.

"She calls this the Day of Mourning, and while I think we can be thankful for what we have, maybe it's better not to call this Thanksgiving or a celebration," I say.

"I respect that," Oliver says.

Everyone else agrees.

"I'm impressed," Tana says to me. "Good for you for speaking up."

It does feel good to speak up. In fact, that makes me think of Dad and how I've been keeping all my feelings inside. Maybe it's time to speak up to him, too.

As we eat, Ryan notes that the school doesn't seem to have skimped for this meal. Maybe we're imagining the money troubles, although I keep thinking about Dr. Ward's ledger.

For dessert there are pumpkin and apple pies, but also an ice cream sundae bar. It's as I'm scooping vanilla ice cream into my bowl that it hits me. On the clue card the word "snow" is printed larger than the other words. We already determined that the final envelope is outdoors, but we need to have a starting point. Snow means winter. I've been walking the trails, and there is a Winter Trail. That's where we're supposed to go. I just know it!

"You've got that look on your face, Mizuno," Zane says when I sit back down with my half-made sundae.

It's unnerving how attentive and quiet he is. Also, how transparent is my face?

Ryan and Tana turn to me, halfway through their desserts. Caleb and Oliver have gone back to their rooms, so it's just the four of us.

"I think we need to be on the Winter Trail, one of the hiking trails here," I explain. "And maybe we'll see an X to mark the hidden room."

I walked that long trail with Carole last week and didn't see an X anywhere, but I wasn't looking for one.

"Excellent," Tana says. "We can go first thing in the morning."

Suddenly the lights flicker, and I notice that it's gotten very dark outside. The wind howls.

"The weather said fifty percent chance of snow," Tana reports. The weather is always posted in the foyer, but she is probably one of the few who actually check it. "It said nothing about a blizzard."

"It definitely looks like a blizzard," Ryan says, staring at the rattling windows.

Miss Jillian steps into the room. "Students need to return to their rooms," she announces. "We may lose power, and though we have an emergency generator, it's only for necessary equipment to run the manor safely. That means minimal lighting. You will have to remain in your rooms until further notice."

Great. This blizzard had better be over by tomorrow.

CHAPTER 60

AS PREDICTED, THE POWER goes out on Thursday night. The generators kick in, but there's only enough power to feed us and keep the living quarters warm. We aren't allowed out of our rooms other than to eat in the state room, where the staff keeps a fire going in the fireplace. The dorm rooms and bathrooms have heat, but the lights are kept low. Tana definitely isn't allowed to use the computer room.

At least we have Sir Grey. He's getting all the attention.

"I'll bet you wish you went home after all," I say to Tana as we bat a ball of paper for Sir Grey on Friday morning after breakfast. He pounces willy-nilly.

Tana shrugs. "I'll see my family for the holidays. At least Hanukkah falls closer to Christmas this year so I can be home for that. Although, I missed the High Holidays."

I feel bad that I didn't even think about that. I remember Addy observing Rosh Hashanah and Yom Kippur. "I'm sorry."

"Don't be," Tana says. "LCA would have allowed me to go home, but my parents and I decided that since I'm doing so well here, I should stay. Education first! That's the Rabin motto."

We pass the time on Friday and then Saturday reading for fun, something neither of us has done so far this school year. I didn't bring any of my manga with me, and we're not even allowed to go to the library, so I settle in with the only non-textbook I have. The book we stole/borrowed from the staff library, *Secrets of English Manors*.

It's actually more interesting than I expected, since I know stuff from Mom's obsession with English things.

"Hey," I say, interrupting Tana's reading. "There's a bit here on Leland Chase."

She comes over to me and peers at the pages. "Really?"

"Yeah. There's a section about this manor. Leland Chase had two sons, like Ms. Sheth said, but only one got married and had children." I skim, running my finger down the page. "I wonder if anyone is left of the family."

"There!" Tana jabs at a paragraph.

"Hmm," I say, reading quickly. "Only one descendant remains. Charles Chase. How new is this book?" I turn to the copyright page. "Oh, this was published last year.

According to this he'd be in his twenties now. I wonder where he is and what he does."

"You can do a search on him on the computer," Tana says. "Or I can."

I point to her. "No way. Ms. Sheth said I would get extra credit but you wouldn't."

"I'm sure she would be fair about it if I came to her with the answers," Tana says. But then she smiles. "Seriously, let's do this together. I'm bored. You can have the extra credit, but let's find out more."

I point to the book. "This is all the information we have."

Tana gets that look in her eyes. "We can get more. I can get more."

"We aren't allowed to use the computer room," I say.

"Since when have we let rules stop us?" Tana says. "Come on. We've been stuck in our room for two days now. Plus, Colette isn't here."

I look at my watch. "Room check in two hours."

Too bad there's no way to get word out to the guys. Not that they'd care about this assignment. Tana and I make our way to the student computer room easily in the dim emergency lighting. We know our way well.

Fortunately, the door is not locked. Tana slides onto the chair at her favorite computer, and I sit next to her. We keep the lights off and our fingers crossed as she boots up the computer.

"There *is* power to the computers," she says. "We could have been using them all along."

"Safety first," I say, imitating Dr. Ward.

As soon as the computer boots up, Tana's fingers fly over the keyboard at super speed. I've been in the room with her before while doing assignments, but I've never paid attention to her as she worked.

She has several windows open, and even as she does a search, before I can even glance at the first lines, she's moved on.

"Stop," I say, trying to read.

"Nope. We're digging, Meg, and nothing that pops up right away is important enough."

I give up, lean back in my chair, and wait. I don't have to wait long.

"Here we go," she says.

I move my chair closer to Tana and squint at the screen. "There's a grandfather still alive," I say, reading quickly. "I wonder why he wasn't mentioned in the book?"

"He's in a residential home," Tana says. "He has dementia. Maybe the family didn't want to mention him because of that? Keep the grandfather's condition a secret?"

"So, the actual truth is that Charles *and* his grandfather are the only living descendants of Leland Chase," I say. I try to read on, but Tana has closed that window and is typing away again. Not on any search engine I've ever seen. In fact, the windows popping up don't look familiar to me at all, and at one point it looks like she's chatting with other people, maybe. I don't ask because I know I won't understand whatever long, complicated explanation Tana might give.

She types for a few more minutes, a look of intense concentration on her face, but also she's smiling. Finally she turns to me.

"Here's something interesting," she says. "This was buried deep. Either it's a false rumor or someone wanted to make sure no one ever saw this."

"What is it?"

"There was a story that Leland Chase hid a treasure here."

"A treasure? What kind of treasure?" My heart beats faster.

Tana shrugs. "I can't find anything more on that. Only that it was meant for his family. Oh, and he apparently kept a diary. Maybe the diary has information about the treasure."

"Another treasure hunt," I say.

"Yeah, but this manor is huge, and without clues or even an idea of what that treasure is, we don't know where to start looking. And we don't know if this story is true."

I tap on the screen. "Any ideas about where that diary is?"

Tana shakes her head. "I've been digging but hit only dead ends."

I glance at the clock on the wall, and my heart leaps. "Fifteen minutes till room check."

"This is enough for extra credit," Tana says.

"We can present it when we're back in class."

"We?" Tana smiles.

"Yeah, we can share the extra credit," I say as Tana closes windows and does some more typing, maybe to erase her trail.

We make it back to our room in time without getting caught. I smile at Tana. A real smile. These couple of days trapped together actually has been a good thing. I feel the connection again between us, and if anything, I've learned that misunderstandings and mistakes happen. And forgiveness is important. Trust is important.

"Hey, Tana?"

Tana pauses in changing into her pj's and turns to me, a question in her eyes.

"What would you say if I suggest we tell Ms. Sheth about Charles Chase and his grandfather but keep the other stuff to ourselves? And of course tell the guys?"

She grins. "For a future adventure?"

I nod.

"Deal!"

But that doesn't really help us for *this* treasure hunt. We only have one more day.

Tana looks out the window into the dark night, where the snow is still falling steadily. "I think it's letting up," she says.

I hope she's right.

CHAPTER 61

WHEN WE WAKE UP on Sunday, we have full power again! The storm is over. Tana and I squeal in delight. Then we look out our window. There is a lot of snow. I can't see any of the benches or shrubs in the yard, and the statues sit atop pedestals of snow. We're going to have to wait for the landscape crew to plow and shovel before we head to the Winter Trail.

At breakfast we four are nearly bouncing out of our skin after being holed up for so long, waiting to finally getting a chance to finish this treasure hunt. The sounds of the loud buzzing of snowblowers and the scraping of plow gives me hope. The four of us decide to head out at noon.

* * *

"It's freezing!" Tana complains for the third time.

"We haven't even gotten to the trailhead yet," I say.

Tana's not much of an outdoor person either, but I guessed that from the beginning. And unfortunately, I haven't had enough sessions with Carole yet to feel competent, so I'm grateful that both Ryan and Zane seem comfortable out here.

Fortunately, the crew has plowed the trails, guessing that we'd want to get outside after being cooped up for nearly three days.

I lead the group to the fountain, and then it's another fifteen minutes till we get to the sign marking the start of the Winter Trail. Tana is panting.

I turn to her, worried. "Are you going to be okay? You can wait for us inside if you want. I promise we'll come get you if we find anything."

"No," she says, leaning her hands on her knees. "I just need a minute to catch my breath."

While we give her a minute (or two), I scan the path. I may not know north from south, but I know my way. Even if the path wasn't cleared, I could find my way on this trail. I send a silent thank-you to Carole for assigning me these trails before the break.

"Okay," Tana says. "I'm ready."

It's as if the weather was listening, because snow starts to fall. Slowly at least.

"We'd better get moving," I say.

"Let's do it," Ryan says.

We troop forward, heads down, because now, of course, the wind is picking up. I'm glad we don't have to be in uniform during break, and I'm glad for my jeans, sweater, and knit cap, plus my down coat. All I can hear (and feel) is the frigid wind and the crunch of our boots as we trek along the path. My breath comes out in puffs of steam, and my eyebrows feel like they are freezing. The temps are dropping.

Snow falls, faster and heavier. Not quite a blizzard, but not a dusting, either. We probably shouldn't be out here, but nobody complains and nobody suggests turning around. Visibility is still good at least. It's not like there will be a sign that says LOOK HERE! IT'S A HIDDEN ROOM, but there *will* be a sign of some sort. I just need to keep my eyes open.

I'm chanting the clue over and over in my head like a mantra. I'm on "X always marks the spot" when I see it.

I stop so suddenly that Tana runs into me and knocks me face-first into a snowbank, falling on top of me.

CHAPTER 62

"SORRY, SORRY!" TANA SAYS, her voice muffled against my back. She struggles to get up.

Arms wrap around my waist and haul me back onto my feet. Ryan is tugging Tana up at the same time. Zane's arms pull away from me, but I can still feel the warmth of them. I mumble my thanks and brush the snow off myself. Tana's cheeks are bright pink, and I suspect it's more from the near hug she got from Ryan than from the cold.

"You two okay?" Ryan asks.

"Yes, thanks," Tana answers brightly.

Zane asks, "Why'd you stop, Mizuno?"

I point. The snow is coming down harder, but the two dark slashes crossed on the wall above barren vines are hard to miss. It's a mosaic embedded into a tall stone wall.

"X marks the spot," Tana breathes.

I smile. "X marks the spot."

The wall is off the trail and piled with snow. I take a step, and my leg sinks in and snow falls into my boots. I'm not sure I can wade through this.

"We've got it," Ryan says. He and Zane take the lead, and Tana and I let them. I'm a feminist for sure, but I'm also not against getting help when I need it. The boys break a path, and after much huffing and puffing we finally make it to the wall.

"Now what?" Tana asks.

"I guess we look for some kind of opening? Or switch?" I say as I start to pat down the wall.

I realize that the Mastermind has to be someone who knows this property well. Otherwise how would they have known about this mosaic? I'm able to identify the wisteria vine, thanks to Carole, who has been teaching me how to identify plants in the winter months. She told me that in the summer these vines are full and lush. This vine would cover the entire wall except in the winter.

"Check the wall and behind the vines," I say.

The snow is falling faster, making it hard to see. I brush snow from the wall and discover that it's not a solid wall after all. There's an opening.

"These are columns," Ryan says next to me.

I push snow away from the opening until it's large enough for me to squeeze through. I take a tentative step, making sure there's actual ground on the other side and not a drop-off. When my boot hits stone, I step in.

"Whoa," I say, and my voice echoes.

Tana, Ryan, and Zane follow. We are in a large chamber with a high stone ceiling.

"This has got to be the place!" Tana exclaims. Her voice bounces off the walls.

There are two stone benches against the far wall and a large empty planter that probably had a tree or something in it long ago.

"It seems abandoned," I say.

"What next?" Ryan asks.

I recite the clue out loud from memory. "You found what was hidden. From ten players to one. You're steps away from winning. Come snow or ice or freezing rain, X always marks the spot, but only for the best."

"We found what was hidden," Tana says, spinning in a slow circle.

"And we used the clues from the last sentence," I say. "The weather elements meant outdoors, and 'snow' meant the Winter Trail."

"And 'X marks the spot,'" Ryan adds.

"So, we need to use the numbers," Zane says softly. "Ten and one."

"And steps," I say slowly. "Those numbers must mean the number of steps to take. But from where?"

I close my eyes, seeing the words on the card. Everyone gets quiet, giving me space.

"Snow" was printed larger to indicate it was important. "Snow" meant the Winter Trail. The *S* in "spot" was capitalized and larger as well. *S* has to stand for something that will help us.

My eyes fly open. "I've got it," I say.

"S IN 'SPOT' WAS capitalized. *S* means 'south,'" I say, still processing. "'You're steps away' means taking steps from the south? And the number might mean ten plus one. Eleven steps."

"Awesome," Ryan says.

"Um," I say with an embarrassed grin. "I have no idea where south is." For the first time since I arrived, I wish we had our cell phones. We'd have a compass.

"Easy," Zane says. He points to the far wall with the benches.

Impressive.

"But where do we start from? That's a long wall."

"Between the benches," Tana says with confidence.

"Why?" Ryan asks.

She shrugs. "Unless Meg has a better idea, it makes the most sense as a starting point. It's just enough room for one person. Or are we missing something?"

"Let's give it a try," I say. It's better than standing here.

Ryan bows and sweeps his arm toward the benches. "You do the honors, Meg."

Here goes nothing, I think. I start with my back to the wall and count eleven steps, trying to take average-size strides. When I get to eleven, I stop on a square of stone. I squat, and the others hurry over to join me. Nothing about this stone looks remarkable. It's filthy with years or maybe even decades of dirt and grime.

I use my mitten to wipe the stone, and the others join in, like our job is to polish it.

"Stop!" Tana shouts. She points to the corner nearest me. There, etched in stone, is a tiny X.

"X marks the spot," I whisper.

"Now what?" Tana asks.

"I think we need to lift it," I say with a groan. I sit down because my legs ache from squatting. I've never been good at the Asian squat like Mom was. She could squat and garden for hours.

"How are we going to lift that?" Tana asks. "It looks heavy."

I run my fingers along the edges. There's a space between the stones, but it's too narrow for my fingers to fit. I'm not giving up. Not when we're so close.

"Huh, check this out."

We all turn to see Zane peering into the giant planter by the benches. He leans in and pulls out a duffel bag. He brings it over and deposits it in front of me. Something clanks.

I unzip the bag, and inside is a crowbar. It's heavy and the cold seeps through my mittens. Gripping it firmly, I wedge it under the bottom edge of the stone square. The crowbar slips in easily, and I lean my weight onto it. I nearly topple over when the stone lifts. It flips over with a big clunk and cracks in two.

"Oops," I say. But my distress is quickly replaced by excitement. There in the dirt is a silver envelope.

And just as quickly my joy turns to anger. Ryan swoops down, snags the envelope, and runs! Runs away from us. From me. With my prize.

CHAPTER 64

"NO!" I SHOUT.

I'm shocked a second time when Tana laughs. Laughs! She's in on this too? I look at her, my heart breaking as I realize that she and Ryan really have conspired against me. She lied to me again and I believed her! Friendships aren't real. She betrayed me. All of these thoughts flit through my head in a second.

And then my keen observation skills kick in. (Because I'm not as observant when I'm emotional.)

Tana is laughing, but so is Ryan. It's happy laughter, not spiteful. I swirl around and see that Ryan isn't running very fast. He's jogging backward, waving the envelope at me, grinning. Teasing. He ducks back through the opening, and Zane surprises me by shouting, "Charge!" like he's a boy playing tag.

Zane rushes past me and flings himself through the opening. I hear Ryan grunt and then muffled laughter. Tana grabs my hand and pulls me out of the chamber. Zane pins Ryan down in a deep snowdrift. Ryan's still laughing, holding the envelope up in the air, keeping it from being buried in the snow. Tana lets go of me and flies into Zane, who topples onto Ryan, who laughs even harder.

Oh, whatever! I join the dog pile, and giggles bubble up in me as I land on Tana, who is shaking with laughter.

"Hey," Ryan calls out, his laughter muffled. "I can't breathe! Get off."

One by one we roll off into the snow until we are lined up on our backs. Our breaths puff into the air above us. Snow seeps under my scarf and coat. My jeans grow damp. But I don't care. I stare up at the clear blue sky. It stopped snowing.

Ryan props himself up, his face hovering over mine. He grins and hands me the envelope.

I don't want to open it sitting in the middle of a snowbank. We're all chilled. I lead the way and walk back to the manor. We're damp, but none of us wants to take the time to change in our rooms. We head straight to the Green Room, where thankfully there's a fire blazing in the fireplace. I unzip my coat, dump it onto the floor, and kick off my boots. The others follow suit. Huddling as close to the fire as we dare, I sigh. It feels so good.

"Ready?" I ask.

"Do it," Ryan says.

I open the flap and pull out the card. Charcoal-colored with silver ink as always. Tana, Ryan, and Zane all stay put even though I expected them to crowd me, trying to see over my shoulder. I could keep this to myself. But we've earned this together.

"Congratulations," I read out loud. "You are the winner! To claim your prize of an all-expenses-paid vacation to Newport Beach over winter break, send your full legal name along with this code to the following email address by Monday at 11:59 p.m. Confirmation with details on your prize to follow."

At the bottom is a code that is simple and straightforward. I AM THE WINNER. The email address is LCA-newportbeach@memail.com.

"You did it!" Tana hugs me.

"Congratulations, Mizuno," Zane says.

Ryan just grins at me.

None of them seems angry or resentful. They all look genuinely happy for me. Oddly, I don't feel as victorious as I thought I would. The Mastermind said "the best" would find X marks the spot. I'm not really the best. I'm only my best with my friends.

CHAPTER 65

THAT EVENING MISS JILLIAN unlocks the door to the sitting room of Dr. Ward's office.

"Just close the door behind you when you're done, and it will automatically lock," she says.

Once Miss Jillian leaves, I sit on the couch and stare at the phone, tapping my fingers on the end table, waiting for the phone to ring. I pace around the couch and get dizzy.

When I pause, I hear voices from outside the office. Needing a distraction and feeling nosy, I walk to the door and press my ear against it.

"I don't like this at all." It's Miss Jillian.

"I know you don't." It's a man's voice, but it sounds distant. Miss Jillian must have her phone on speaker.

"If I get caught—" she starts to say.

"It's all for a good cause." The man cuts her off.

"You promise?" she asks, lowering her voice.

"Baby, when have I ever steered you wrong?"

Miss Jillian has a boyfriend! It's weird to think of the adults at LCA having lives outside of school. The voices fade, and I can't hear clearly anymore. Miss Jillian must have walked away. I no longer have that phone call to distract me from the one I'm about to have. I'm full of nerves because I need to have a difficult conversation with my dad.

Dad's on time as always, but when the phone rings, I jump.

I answer before the second ring. "Hi, Dad," I say breathlessly.

"Megumi! Happy belated Thanksgiving! I hope you had a delicious meal over there," he says, his voice warm.

"I did. Six of us stayed at the manor, and it's been fun."

There's a short pause before Dad says, "You sound good, Megumi. Happy. I'm glad. Going to that school has been good for you."

He's right. It has. But being happy doesn't mean I'm ready to forget my sadness over losing Mom. It's clear now that no matter how badly I want Dad to be able to read my mind, he can't. I have to tell him how I feel, as hard as it is, because if I don't at least try, that means I've given up. One thing I learned from Mom's treasure hunts is to never give up.

"Dad, I have some things I want to talk to you about."

"Okay?" Dad sounds less sure now.

"Hear me out, please?"

"Of course."

He says it like he's surprised I even have to ask, but since Mom died, he hasn't really listened to me at all.

I speak quickly because I'm afraid I'll lose my nerve or that Dad will cut me off. "I miss Mom, and I know you do too. But she's gone. I'm sad about it. Really sad. But there's nothing we can do about it. I mean, we can't bring her back. But I miss you, too, Dad."

"Megumi." Dad's voice is soft.

"I don't want you to sell the house," I say. "I don't want you to throw away all the memories we have of Mom."

Dad doesn't say anything, so I barrel on.

"You never traveled so much when Mom was around. Why don't you want to be around me, Dad? Why did you send me away to Aunt Vivian's? To LCA? Why do you leave all the time?" And now the tears flow. I can't stop them. I hiccup and sniffle.

"Megumi," Dad says, his voice tight. Is he angry? "I'm so sorry. I feel horrible. I didn't mean to make you feel like I abandoned you. I've been grieving, but I see that it's been in a very unhealthy way."

I wipe my nose on my cardigan sleeve. Why aren't there any tissues in this room?

"I won't sell the house," he says.

"You won't?"

"It's been hard, being in the house without you and without Mom. But you're right, Megumi." Dad clears his throat. "We can make new memories, you and me. We're still a family."

I start crying again, but this time because I'm relieved and happy. "I can come home? You'll stop traveling?"

"You're unhappy there?" Dad asks.

It's hard to admit this, but since I'm working hard to be honest with Dad, I can't bring myself to lie. "I'm not miserable, no."

"I would like to travel less," Dad says, "but I can't quit this position in the middle of my projects. It will take me some time to close out these deals and see if I can get a new position in the company that keeps me at home again, like before."

"Oh."

"If we can convince Aunt Vivian to move to our house, at least until I can travel less, maybe we can work something out so you can go to the middle school in our district."

Oh no. Not Aunt Vivian. Also, if I attend the middle school at home, I'll have to face Addy again. I'd start school in the middle of the year with no friends. I have friends here at LCA. It feels strange to realize this, but I'm not ready to leave. Not yet. Now that I know that Dad won't sell the house and he plans to travel less soon, I don't feel so anxious.

"Actually, maybe I can finish out the school year here," I say. "If that's okay."

"That would be great, Megumi! By the time you're done with seventh grade, I'm sure I'll be home more. You can move home this summer. Does that sound good?"

"That sounds great, Dad!" And little does he know that I'll have a nice surprise of a vacation for us this Christmas.

"I promise to do better," Dad says. "To be your dad and to be your family. I'm sorry I've been away for so long."

I know he doesn't mean his business travel. "I know, Dad. Thanks."

"I do love you, you know," he says quietly.

"I love you too, Dad."

CHAPTER 66

ON MONDAY MORNING LCA is back to business as usual. The dining room is crowded with all thirty-five of us, and everyone shares stories from break. The noise level is higher than usual. I check behind me, and Colette is eating quietly.

"Have you sent the email yet?" Ryan asks.

I shake my head. "I'll wait until study hall," I say. The only reason I haven't sent it off yet is that I've been contemplating a plan. I think I'm ready to share it with my friends. "But I have an idea."

"Oh?" Tana says.

"Meet me in our secret room before Life Skills," I say.

Tana checks her watch. "We can't be tardy."

"Then you'd better be quick," I say as I get up to bus

my dishes. I purposely walk by the other row of tables and stop at Colette.

"Hey," I say. "Good break?"

She looks up at me and then glances around, as if I might be talking to someone else. She gives me a tentative smile. "Yeah."

"Cool," I say. Then I dump my dishes and head straight to the storage room with our secret hideout.

Before I can open the panel, I hear footsteps, and I freeze, wondering if Colette followed. But no, it's just my friends. They smile when they see me.

We quickly duck into our room. Jung may have claimed the hidden room on the fourth floor, but this one is ours. When we're all sitting, I place the last clue card on the floor.

"There's no way I could have gotten this without you all. In fact, the four of us worked together from the very start. We all won. We should all claim this prize," I say.

"But how would that even work?" Ryan asks.

"We could each send the email," I say. "Or maybe just send one and sign all our names to it?"

There's a long silence as we all contemplate.

"Or," Tana says.

We all swing to her. She has that look on her face that she has whenever she talks about computers.

"I could create a program that will send emails from

each one of us at exactly the same time. With the exact same time stamp. It would be a four-way tie."

"That's brilliant, Tana," I say.

"I don't know," Zane says.

"You don't know if Tana can do it?" I ask. "She can!"

"Yeah, she can do it," Zane says. "But what if we all get disqualified? I mean, paying for a trip for one person is one thing, but adding three more is a lot of extra money."

"He's probably loaded," Ryan says. "How else could he have managed this whole thing?"

"Don't be so sure it's not a woman," Tana points out.

Zane keeps talking. "Like I said before when this all started, something is off. Who does something like this? Who gives away big prizes for no return? What's the catch?"

"I know what you mean," Tana says. "The whole keeping-this-quiet thing is a little disturbing."

"Who is the Mastermind, anyway?" I ask, frowning. "I mean, what's their endgame? At first it felt like this was a fun activity for the students, but it doesn't really feel like that anymore."

"It's creepy how this person seems to know stuff about us," Zane adds. "And whoever it is knows this campus and manor."

"I've been thinking about that," I say. "It could be anyone." I even briefly wondered if it could be Carole. She's conveniently away a lot, and she led me to study the trails. But it makes no sense for her to do something like that. Like Zane said, what would be her goal?

"Yeah, okay, it's a mystery for sure," Ryan says. "But if there really is a prize of a vacation, then it can't be bad, can it?"

"Well, I know," Zane says, "nothing is free."

"Are you saying you don't think we should claim the prize?" Ryan asks.

He shakes his head. "It's up to Mizuno."

"We've worked too hard," I say. "We deserve this."

"Meg needs this prize so her dad won't sell her house," Ryan says.

I do still need the vacation. Not because I have to convince Dad anymore, but it would be nice to go away with him and for him to meet my friends. We deserve a getaway.

I turn to Tana. "How sure are you that you can get all four emails to have the exact same time stamp?"

"I'm one hundred percent sure," she says with confidence.

I look at my friends. "I had a really good talk with my dad last night. He's not selling the house. And he's going to try to travel less. I might be able to move home this summer."

"You're leaving?" Tana asks, her face full of surprise.

Oh right. No one knew I was trying to get home permanently. All I told them was that I needed to convince my dad not to sell the house.

"Well, it's not for sure," I say. "And that's not the point! I think we should all claim the prize. I think we should all go to Newport Beach together. I'm willing to risk being disqualified. And if we can manage this, I can still ask my dad to chaperone. It's win-win-win!"

Everyone smiles and nods.

"You've got till study hall," I say to Tana.

"No problem. I'll work on it during IS," she says. "Meet me at the computer room during study hall."

The day drags.

Finally it's time, and I hurry to the computer room. Ryan used his charm to convince Ms. Sheth to let us four study in the computer room without supervision. I don't know how he does it, but I'm glad he's on our side.

"Well?" Ryan asks as soon as we barge into the computer room.

Tana grins. "Sit down at a computer and log into your email account."

Zane and Ryan sit at computers by the windows, and I sit next to Tana. Once we compose our notes to the Mastermind, Tana has us send our emails to her account. We gather behind her to watch her screen.

"Ready?" Tana's finger hovers over the enter key.

"Set?" Ryan says.

"Go!" I say.

Whoosh. Our emails go to the Mastermind.

And now we wait.

CHAPTER 67

IT'S BEEN FOUR DAYS since we sent off our emails to the Mastermind. Every morning after breakfast we meet in the computer room to check our email accounts. Nothing. Every evening after lights-out we stare at the crack under our dorm room doors, willing an envelope to appear. Nothing. We try hard to focus on our classes and assignments. But we are very distracted.

"If this keeps up," Tana says during game night on Friday, "I'm going to do very poorly during finals."

Ryan barks a laugh. "As if."

"You'd think if we were going to be disqualified, they would have let us know by now," I muse as I move my game piece five spaces ahead.

"Maybe the silence is a message," Tana says, drawing

a card. "Maybe that's the way we know that none of us has won."

"Or maybe the Mastermind just wants us to suffer," Zane says.

"What is wrong with you four?" Colette walks over to us. "Everyone else is done with their game, but you all are still in the middle of it. Less talk. More fun. When I come back in twenty minutes, you'd better be cleaning up."

Well, at least she isn't threatening demerits for us not being better at having fun.

We are the only students remaining. Once we are sure Colette has left, I gather the game pieces and toss them into the box.

"Hey!" Zane protests. "I was winning!"

Tana reveals the card she drew, which would have sent his piece back to the start. "Not for long, though."

He huffs in frustration and takes the stack of cards and returns it to the game box.

"I have an idea," I say. "I don't think the Mastermind is going to not have a winner to this game. There's a point to this, and, like Zane, I don't think it's all fun and games." At least not anymore.

Tana frowns.

I continue. "Don't you want to know who the Mastermind is?"

My friends all nod, but Tana looks nervous.

"I don't know," she says. "This sounds risky."

Zane says, "I'm in. I don't like being manipulated. Even if the prize is real, I'd like to know who's running this game. And why."

"Well, I don't know about figuring out why right away, but we can figure out who," I say.

"How?" Ryan asks.

"I'm going to hide in the bathroom after lights-out," I say. "If I hear footsteps, I'll peek out and see who it is."

"You're going to wait in the bathroom all night?" Tana squeaks.

"We can't very well yank our door open when the envelope comes and let the Mastermind know we're onto them," I say.

"Cuz we still want the prize," Ryan says.

"That too," I say. But if this truly isn't all fun and games, like Zane said, I want to know who the Mastermind is and possibly figure out the reason for this treasure hunt.

That night after lights-out, I head to the bathroom. Kylie is at the sink washing her hands. We nod to each other, and when she leaves, I stand with my ear near the door, hoping that whoever the Mastermind is, they aren't as silent when walking as Zane is.

I wait and wait and wait. I glance at my watch. It's only been an hour. I shift back and forth on my feet. But then I hear footsteps! I brace myself in case it's a classmate heading to the bathroom. The footsteps pass the door. My heart pounds in my ears. I don't want to open the door too early, but I also don't want to be too late.

The footsteps pause, and I hold my breath. When I hear the creak of the floor, I slowly ease the door open and peek out.

There, walking away past Colette's room, is Miss Jillian! Doing her rounds? Or is she the Mastermind?

Once she disappears around the corner away from the girls' wing, I hurry back to my room. Tana sits on my bed, holding two envelopes.

CHAPTER 68

"DID YOU SEE WHO it was?" Tana whispers as I sit down next to her. She hands me an envelope with my name on it, and she has one with hers.

"It was Miss Jillian," I say softly.

"Miss Jillian?" Tana gasps. "She's the Mastermind? But why?"

My thoughts exactly. What's in it for her? She's new, so maybe she took the job to run a treasure hunt? But why? Is she secretly rich? She is the nicest of the security staff. Is she, like, some kind of fairy godmother type?

But it kind of makes sense. I think back to those items in the treasure chest and how mine was a plastic dinosaur. Miss Jillian did the bag checks when I first arrived. She would have gone into my duffel bag and seen everything in it, all the treasures from Mom. She has access to student files, and she can hide things not only on the student side of the manor but also on the administration side. And she's the one who caught Zane and Ryan when we were breaking into the staff library. Maybe that's why she didn't turn them in, because she's behind the whole treasure hunt.

Tana nudges me out of my thoughts. "Are we going to open them?"

We each take a deep breath and pull out the familiar charcoal-colored cards.

Cleverness can sometimes be rewarded,
or punished.
All four will take the prize,
this time.
A new game awaits you.
There will be only one winner declared by me.
Because there must be only one winner to claim
the title of BEST Treasure Hunter.
I may not be at LGA or in Newport Beach,
but I have eyes everywhere.
Do not cheat, & no more working together.
Below is your itinerary.
Get ready for the real game.
~The Mastermind

"Another game?" Tana says.

"Wait. It can't be Miss Jillian," I say, peering closer at my card. "It says 'I may not be at LCA . . . but I have eyes everywhere.'"

"That's seriously creepy." Tana drops her card like it might bite her.

"Eyes everywhere," I repeat. I turn to Tana. "I heard Miss Jillian talking to her boyfriend on the phone. She was saying something about how she was worried she was going to get caught."

Tana blinks at me, her mouth open.

"So maybe she's not the Mastermind, but she's totally working for him, whoever he is."

"What are we going to do?" Tana asks.

I lean over, pick up her card, and hand it back to her. "We're going to play."

And I'm going to find out who the Mastermind is and what he wants.

ACKNOWLEDGMENTS

To my agent Tricia Lawrence. A decade and over a dozen books later, thanks for taking a chance on me and believing in my stories. You are a savvy career manager and a cherished friend who always has my back!

To my editor, Aly Heller, who was enthusiastic about Last Chance Academy from the beginning. Thank you for your guidance and fun brainstorming sessions. I can't wait to continue exploring the LCA manor and grounds with you!

Having a writing career is a dream come true. It is an honor to get to write books for young people. A big shout-out to anyone who has taken time to read my books, write to me, and/or come to my events (including the reader who was so excited she forgot to put on her shoes). You, the readers, keep me going! Thank you to the educators, librarians, parents, and booksellers for putting books into readers' hands. A special thank-you to Aliza Werner, who was the first teacher back in 2017 to reach out to tell me how my book made a difference for one of her third graders.

Big hugs and thanks to the following friends for being on my team and offering support, advice, and/or answering my queries (although any mistakes in the book are my own): Jenne Abramowitz, Nova Lee & Willow Andree,

ACKNOWLEDGMENTS

Lynn Bauer, Winsome Bingham, Josie Cameron, Sarah Park Dahlen, Cindy Faughnan, Betina Hsieh, Mike Jung, Jung Kim, Jo Knowles, Carole Lindstrom, Kashmira Sheth, Christina Soontornvat, Susan Tan, Andrea Wang, and Paula Yoo. Gratitude to Karina Yan Glaser for our New Puppy Mama Club chats. And a fast and furious thank-you to Grace Lin for 997 miles driven together on our first Very Asian Book (and Boba Tea) Trip. What a fun adventure!

While I'm grateful to be able to write in my studio, the Word Nest, with my rescue dogs, Kiku and Ponyo, getting away for writing retreats has been vital to meeting deadlines and starting new projects. Thank you, Kristy Boyce and Dr. Holly Carter, for the writing retreat at Harlaxton Manor in England in 2022. Not only did I work on a draft of this book there, but the manor and secret rooms served as inspirations for Leland Chase Academy. Huge thanks to George Brown and the Highlights Foundation staff for providing a magical retreat space (and delicious meals). And thanks also to Annie Philbrick for the Book Nook.

Thank you to the amazing team at Aladdin: Valerie Garfield, Kristin Gilson, Anna Jarzab, Heather Palisi, Art Morgan, Sara Berko, Bara MacNeill, Valerie Shea, and cover illustrator August Zhang. I'm so happy to have you all on Team LCA!

I'm especially grateful to my family, who always support and encourage me. I love you all! Thanks to my husband, Bob Florence, who never wavered in his belief in me, and to my daughter, Caitlin Schumacher, who is my biggest cheerleader. Also much gratitude to my sister, Gail Hirokane; my brother-in-law, John Parkison; my niece, Laurel Parkison; and my son and daughter-in-law, Jason and Samala Florence. An extra-big thank-you to my late father, Denta Hirokane, for reading to me as a child and to my mom, Yasuko Hirokane Fordiani, for all those trips to the library and fostering my love for writing. A very special thank-you to my late stepdad, Bob Fordiani, for love, laughter, and generosity. I miss you. I hope wherever you are, you are getting to sit on the beach, eat all the pasta, and read all the books.

ABOUT THE AUTHOR

Debbi Michiko Florence is the author of more than twenty-five books for children and tweens, including the Jasmine Toguchi chapter book series. A third-generation Japanese American, Debbi was born and raised in California and now calls Connecticut home. When she's not writing in her studio (the Word Nest), she enjoys reading, playing with her rescue dogs, watching J-dramas and anime, and traveling with her husband and daughter.